THE NEW WINDMILL BOOK OF
STORIES FROM OTHER TIMES

EDITED BY LOUISE NAYLOR

F

M003395

Heinemann
New Windmills

Heinemann Educational Publishers
Halley Court, Jordan Hill, Oxford OX2 8EJ
A division of Reed Educational and Professional Publishing Ltd

OXFORD   MADRID   ATHENS   FLORENCE   PRAGUE   CHICAGO
PORTSMOUTH NH (USA)   MEXICO CITY   SÃO PAULO   SINGAPORE
KUALA LUMPUR   TOKYO   MELBOURNE   AUCKLAND   NAIROBI
KAMPALA   IBADAN   GABORONE   JOHANNESBURG

2001 2000 99 98 97
10 9 8 7 6 5 4 3 2 1

ISBN 0 435 12479 X

Acknowledgements
The author and publisher should like to thank the following for permission
to use copyright material:
Macmillan General Books for 'The Thieves who Couldn't Help Sneezing'
by Thomas Hardy; 'The Blue Carbuncle' from *The Adventures of Sherlock
Holmes* by Sir Arthur Conan Doyle. Copyright Northolme Ltd. Reproduced
by kind permission of Jonathan Clowes Ltd, London, on behalf of
Northolme Ltd; The Society of Authors as the literary representative of
the Estate of W W Jacobs for 'The Monkey's Paw' by W W Jacobs.
Every effort has been made to contact the copyright holders. We should
be glad to rectify any omissions at the next reprint if notice is given to the
publisher.

Cover illustration by Chris Cody
Cover design: The Point
Illustrations by GRAF Design (Jane Bottomley)
Typeset by Books Unlimited (Nottm) NG19 7QZ
Printed and bound in the United Kingdom by Clays Ltd, St Ives plc

Contents

Introduction

This collection of stories contains some of the best tales from great writers of the nineteenth century. They have been especially chosen because they are exciting and enjoyable to read.

As you encounter the unexpected plots and vivid characters you may find you want to read the stories many times. Each time you will make new discoveries and meet hidden depths.

You can compare and contrast the stories under the headings suggested, or you may prefer to choose your own themes or read individual stories. Each story has:

- a short introduction, including information about the author's life and times
- glossary boxes, to explain difficult words or phrases
- activities at the end, to help you get to grips with the stories.

In these stories you will meet larger-than-life characters such as Sherlock Holmes and Napoleon Bonaparte. Chilling tales concerning the monkey's paw and the signalman will keep you in suspense. You will discover what motivates people to revenge or murder but also to warmth and self-sacrifice. These stories contain all the elements of life here and now. Generosity, love and heroism stand side by side with murder, mystery and revenge.

Louise Naylor

The Necklace

Guy de Maupassant, 1853–1893

Guy de Maupassant lived in France. As he grew up, he experienced a life of relative wealth and luxury. When war broke out his family lost their fortune and he soon came to know the other side of life – that of poverty and need. Maupassant's stories always contain clever twists and colourful characters.

In the following story Madame Loisel wishes for a luxurious lifestyle that she cannot afford. Then she has an unexpected chance to attend a society ball in a new gown and jewels. But will the experience bring the happiness she longs for?

She was one of those pretty and charming girls, who had been born by an unlucky twist of fate into a lower middle-class family. She had no **dowry**, no hope of inheriting any money, and it was unlikely that she would ever meet a man of wealth and social position who might appreciate her, love her and marry her. And so she allowed herself to be married to a junior clerk in the Ministry of Public Instruction.

She did not have enough money for expensive clothes or jewellery, so she dressed simply. She was unhappy, feeling that she was destined for better things in life. A woman should have no social class; her place in society should depend upon her beauty, her

---

dowry: money paid by the bride's father to her husband's family

1

grace and her charm. If she possessed a natural sense of **refinement**, instinctive good taste and an agile mind, a woman from quite an ordinary family should be able to compete with the grandest lady in the land.

She fretted constantly, feeling that she had been born for all the luxuries and finer things of life. She resented her humble surroundings; the bare walls, the shabby furniture, the ugly fabrics. She was tormented and angered by these things, though another woman of her class would not have even noticed them. Even the sight of her little Breton maid doing the housework aroused in her feelings of hopeless longing for things that could never be. She dreamt of hushed **ante-chambers**, the oriental hangings lit by tall, bronze candelabra, and of two imposing footmen in knee-britches, slumbering in great armchairs by the drowsy heat of the stove. She dreamt of magnificent drawing rooms, furnished with ancient silks, fine antiques and priceless ornaments, and of chic, **perfumed boudoirs**, ideal for afternoon conversation with one's closest friends; or with those fashionable gentlemen that every woman longs to entertain.

When she and her husband sat down to eat at the round dining table, and he took the lid off the soup tureen, exclaiming delightedly, 'Ah, beef stew, my favourite', she would look at the three-day-old cloth and dream of elegant dinner parties. She would picture the gleaming silver on the table, and imagine tapestries adorning the walls with **mythical** scenes. She would dream of eating delicacies served on **exquisite porcelain**, and of accepting whispered compliments with an **enigmatic** smile, whilst she savoured the pink flesh of a trout or the plump wing of a **pullet**.

She had no elegant clothes, no jewels, nothing. Yet she desired nothing else. She felt that she was meant for a life of fashion. She longed to be attractive, to be envied, to be surrounded by admirers.

She had a rich friend from her school days, but she stopped going to visit her. It was so painful to return from her friend's fine home to her own poor apartment that she would fall into a deep depression and cry for days afterwards.

Then, one evening, her husband came home proudly holding a large envelope. She tore it open and took out a printed card on which were the words, 'The Minister of Public Instruction and Madame Georges Ramponneau request the pleasure of the company of Monsieur and Madame Loisel at the Ministry on Monday the 18th of January.'

Instead of the delight which her husband had expected, she threw the invitation on to the table and muttered peevishly, 'And what do you expect me to do about it?'

'But, my dear, I thought you'd be happy. You never get the chance to go out, and this is a real occasion. I went to a lot of trouble to get this invitation. They're really hard to come by. Everyone wants one and they don't give many to junior clerks. Anybody who *is* anybody will be there.'

She glanced at him irritably and snapped, 'And just what do you think I am going to wear to this ball?'

---

refinement: elegance

ante-chambers: hallways, entrance rooms

perfumed boudoirs: scented ladies' rooms

mythical: fairy-tale

exquisite porcelain: delicate and beautiful china

enigmatic: secretive

pullet: young, tender chicken

This was not something that he had even thought of.

He stammered, 'Well, the dress you go to the theatre in. It seems very nice to me . . .'

He lapsed into a stunned silence, lost for words, when he saw that his wife was crying. Two large tears were running slowly down her face.

'But . . . but what's wrong, what's wrong with you?'

With a supreme effort, she overcame her emotions, and, drying her tears, she replied calmly, 'Nothing. It's simply that I have nothing to wear and so I cannot possibly go to this ball. It would be better if you gave the invitation to a colleague whose wife is better dressed than I am.'

Her husband was distressed by this, and replied, 'Look, Mathilde, how much would a suitable dress cost; something simple that you could wear again afterwards?'

She thought it over for a few seconds, taking into account the amount of money they had, and calculating the sum she could ask for without shocking her cautious husband into dismissing the idea out of hand.

At last she replied, hesitantly, 'I'm not exactly sure, but I think that I could manage with four hundred francs.'

He paled slightly, because that was the exact sum that he was saving to buy a gun, so that he could go lark-shooting with his friends, on Sundays during the summer.

In spite of this, he said, 'All right. I'll give you four hundred francs. But try to buy yourself a really beautiful dress.'

As the day of the ball drew nearer, Madame Loisel still seemed downcast and anxious, although her new dress was ready.

'What's wrong? You've been in a strange mood for three days,' her husband asked her one evening.

'I haven't got a single piece of jewellery; not one stone to wear. It would almost be better not to go to this party at all.'

'Why not wear fresh flowers? They are particularly fashionable this season. For ten francs you could buy two or three lovely roses.'

She remained unconvinced.

'No, there is nothing more humiliating than to be poor when you are surrounded by rich women.'

Suddenly, her husband exclaimed, 'How silly you are! Go and see your friend Madame Forestier and ask her if you can borrow some of her jewellery! You know her well enough for that.'

She cried out in delight. 'You're right! Why didn't I think of it myself?'

The next day, she went to see her friend and told her about the problem. Madame Forestier went to a glass-fronted cabinet and produced a large jewellery case. Opening it, she said, 'Choose what you like, my dear.'

First, Madame Loisel saw some bracelets and a pearl necklace, then she saw a Venetian cross, delicately worked in gold and precious stones. She tried the jewels on in front of the mirror and hesitated, unable either to take them off, or to put them back in the box.

All the time she kept asking, 'Have you anything else?'

'Of course, of course. Just carry on looking. I don't know exactly what you want.'

Suddenly, she came across a superb diamond necklace in a black satin case, and her heart began to beat wildly. As she picked it up, her hands shook. She put it on over her high-necked dress and stared at herself in ecstasy.

'Could you lend me this? Just this and nothing else?' she asked, hesitantly.

'Yes, of course.'

She threw her arms round her friend's neck, kissing her delightedly, then rushed home with her prize.

The day of the party arrived. Madame Loisel was the Belle of the Ball. She was the prettiest woman there; elegant and graceful; smiling and vivacious. She attracted the gaze of all the men, who wanted to know who she was and who tried to get themselves introduced to her. All the top ministry officials wanted to dance with her. Even the Minister himself noticed her.

She danced with abandon, carried away on a cloud of happiness, where nothing mattered to her except the sweetness of the triumph that she had longed for.

It was four in the morning when she left the dance floor. Since midnight, her husband had been asleep in the adjoining room, with three other gentlemen whose wives were still enjoying themselves.

As they prepared to go home, Monsieur Loisel draped round her shoulders the cloak she wore every day. The elegance of her ball gown emphasized its dowdiness, and she was suddenly brought down to earth. All she wanted was to leave as quickly as possible, so that she would not be seen by the other women, who were wrapping themselves in rich furs.

Loisel called, 'Wait a moment. It's cold outside. I'll get a carriage.'

She wouldn't listen to him and ran down the steps. Once they were in the street, they found that all the carriages were taken, so they started to hail the passing coachmen, looking for one that was free.

Shivering and disheartened, they made their way towards the River Seine. Eventually, they found an ancient cab down by the riverside. It was one of those ramshackle vehicles that you only see in Paris at night,

Madame Loisel was the Belle of the Ball

as if they were ashamed to reveal their shabbiness in the cold light of day.

It took them to the door of their house in the Rue des Martyrs, and they dejectedly climbed the stairs. For her, it was all over. His only thought was that he had to be at the office by ten o'clock. She took off her cloak and stood once more in front of the mirror to see herself in all her glory. But suddenly she cried out. Her neck was bare. The diamond necklace had gone!

Her husband, already half undressed, asked, 'What's the matter?'

She turned to him in horror.

'The necklace. It's gone!'

'What do you mean? How? It's not possible!'

They searched everywhere. In the folds of her dress, in the pleats of her cloak, in her pockets, but they found nothing.

'Are you sure you had it when you left the ball?' he asked.

'Yes, I remember touching it as we were leaving.'

'But we would have heard it if it had fallen off in the street. You must have lost it in the carriage.'

'Yes, that must be what happened. Can you remember the number?'

'No, did you notice it?'

'No.'

They stared at each other in dismay. Finally, Loisel got dressed again.

'I'll go back over the route where we walked and see if I can find it.'

He went out. Still in her evening dress, she sank in a chair, her mind and body numb with shock. Her husband returned at about seven o'clock in the morning. He had found nothing.

He went to the police station, to the newspapers, to the cab companies; everywhere that might have given them a glimmer of hope. She waited at home all day in the same state of shock, contemplating the terrible disaster. Loisel returned at about seven that evening, his face pale and drawn. There was no trace.

'You must write to your friend and tell her that you have broken the clasp and that you are having it mended. That will give us the time to think of something.'

After a week had passed, they had lost all hope of ever finding the necklace. Loisel, who now looked five years older, said, 'We'll just have to think of a way to replace it.'

So the next day, they took the case that it had come in, and went to the jewellers whose name was inside the lid. He consulted his books.

'I'm afraid that I did not sell this necklace. I must have only supplied the case.'

Sick with anxiety, they went from jeweller to jeweller, searching for a necklace like the one that had been lost, trying hard to remember exactly what it had looked like.

Eventually, in a small shop in the Palais Royal, they found a diamond necklace which seemed to be identical to the one they had lost. It was worth 40,000 francs, but the jeweller said he would let them have it for 36,000.

They persuaded him to keep it for them for three days, on condition that he would buy it from them for 34,000 francs if they should find the original before the end of February. Loisel had 18,000 francs which his father had left him and he would just have to borrow the rest.

He borrowed a thousand francs from one person, five hundred from another; five louis here, three louis there. He wrote IOUs, borrowed money at outrageous rates of interest, dealing with all kind of **unscrupulous** moneylenders. He mortgaged the rest of his life, signing documents without knowing if he would ever be able to honour the debts. He was panic-stricken at the prospect of the physical hardship, mental torture and black despair that he faced in the future, but finally, he went to collect the necklace, putting the 36,000 francs on the counter.

When Madame Loisel returned the necklace, Madame Forestier said coldly, 'You should have brought it back sooner. I might have needed it.'

She didn't open the case as her friend had feared she might. What if she had noticed the change? What would she have thought? What would she have said? Would she have thought that Madame Loisel had stolen it?

Madame Loisel came to know the life of the very poor. She resigned herself bravely to the inevitable. The terrible debt had to be paid and she would pay it. They got rid of the maid and moved to cheaper lodgings, renting an attic room.

She did all the heavy housework and the dirty kitchen jobs. She washed all the dishes, breaking her pink finger nails on the crockery and greasy saucepans. She washed the dirty linen, the shirts and the dish-cloths, hanging them out to dry on the line. Every morning, she took the rubbish down to the street and carried the water back up the stairs, stopping to catch her breath on each landing. She dressed like a working woman, and with her basket on her arm, she bargained with the greengrocer, the grocer and the butcher, braving their insults in order to eke out, penny by penny, her pitiful housekeeping money.

Every month she had to pay off some debts, whilst others were renewed to buy more time. In the evenings, her husband kept the books for a tradesman, and often at night, he did copywriting for five **sou** a page.

And so their lives continued for ten years. At the end of that time, they had paid everything back; everything, including all the **interest that had accrued**.

Madame Loisel looked like an old woman now. She had become strong, hard and coarse, like the women you find in the homes of the poor. She would scrub the floors, talking at the top of her voice, heedless of her uncombed hair, her disordered skirts and her red hands. But sometimes, when her husband was at the office, she would sit at the window and dream of that evening which now seemed to belong to another time; of that ball, when she had been so beautiful and so much admired.

What would her life have been like if she had not lost that necklace? Who could say? Who could know? How strange life is. How suddenly things change! It takes so little to turn happiness into despair.

One Sunday, she had gone for a stroll in the **Champs Elysées** to get away from her everyday cares and worries. Suddenly, she caught sight of a woman and child walking along together. It was Madame Forestier, still young, still beautiful, still attractive.

---

unscrupulous: without conscience, hard hearted

sou: French coin of little value

interest that had accrued: extra payments which had built up

Champs Elysées: fashionable street in Paris

Madame Loisel was overcome with emotion. Should she go and speak to her? Yes, of course, now that she'd paid off the debt, she'd tell her everything. Why not?

She went up to her.

'Hello, Jeanne.'

The other woman showed no sign of recognition, but looked astonished that this common female should address her by her first name.

She stammered, 'But Madame . . . I don't know . . . you must have mistaken me for someone else.'

'No. I am Mathilde Loisel.'

Her friend uttered a cry.

'Oh, my poor Mathilde. How you have changed!'

'Yes. Life has been hard since I last saw you. I've had my fair share of suffering . . . and it's all because of you.'

'Because of me . . . what do you mean?'

'Do you remember lending me that diamond necklace to go to the party at the Ministry?'

'Yes . . . what about it?'

'Well, I lost it!'

'What? But you gave it back to me.'

'I gave you back another one, exactly like it, and it's taken ten years to pay for it. I'm sure you will understand that it wasn't easy for us, because we had nothing. Anyway, it's done now, and I'm glad it's over.'

Madame Forestier had stopped in her tracks.

'Are you telling me that you bought a diamond necklace to replace the one I lent you?'

'Yes, and you didn't notice, did you? They were exactly the same.'

She smiled with simple pride and joy.

Deeply moved, Madame Forestier took both her hands.

'Oh, my poor Mathilde. My necklace was paste. It was worth five hundred francs at most . . .'

Madame Loisel discovers the truth

The Sexton's Hero

Elizabeth Gaskell, 1810–1865

Elizabeth Gaskell's father was a church minister, so she was brought up to be kind and considerate to others. She later married a minister and spent a great deal of time helping the poor in the countryside and in Manchester, where she lived. Elizabeth always believed in people's basic desire to be kind to others. This faith in people's goodness is often reflected in her stories.

When strong, handsome Gilbert Dawson moves to the village of Lindal he quickly becomes popular. But when Letty starts to fall in love with him, it causes problems which have dramatic consequences . . .

The afternoon sun shed down his glorious rays on the grassy churchyard, making the shadow, cast by the old yew-tree under which we sat, seem deeper and deeper by contrast. The everlasting hum of **myriads** of summer insects made luxurious lullaby.

Of the view that lay beneath our gaze, I cannot speak adequately. The foreground was the grey-stone wall of the vicarage-garden; rich in the colouring made by innumerable lichens, ferns, ivy of most tender green and most delicate tracery, and the vivid scarlet of the crane's-bill, which found a home in every nook and crevice – and at the summit of that old wall flaunted some unpruned tendrils of the vine, and long flower-laden branches of the climbing rose-tree, trained against the inner side. Beyond, lay meadow green, and mountain grey, and the blue dazzle of

Morecambe Bay, as it sparkled between us and the more distant view.

For a while we were silent, living in sight and murmuring sound. Then Jeremy took up our conversation where, suddenly feeling weariness, as we saw that deep green shadowy resting-place, we had ceased speaking a quarter of an hour before.

It is one of the luxuries of holiday-time that thoughts are not rudely shaken from us by outward violence of hurry and busy impatience, but fall maturely from our lips in the sunny leisure of our days. The stock may be bad, but the fruit is ripe.

'How would you then define a hero?' I asked.

There was a long pause, and I had almost forgotten my question in watching a cloud-shadow floating over the far-away hills, when Jeremy made answer:

'My idea of a hero is one who acts up to the highest idea of duty he has been able to form, no matter at what sacrifice. I think that by this definition, we may include all phases of character, even to the heroes of old, whose sole (and to us, low) idea of duty consisted in personal **prowess**.'

'Then you would even admit the military heroes?' asked I.

'I would; with a certain kind of pity for the circumstances which had given them no higher ideas of duty. Still, if they sacrificed self to do what they sincerely believed to be right, I do not think I could deny them the title of hero.'

'A poor, unchristian heroism, whose **manifestation** consists in injury to others!' I said.

---

myriads: countless
prowess: bravery
manifestation: evidence, proof

We were both startled by a third voice.

'If I might make so bold, sir' – and then the speaker stopped.

It was the Sexton, whom, when we first arrived, we had noticed, as an accessory to the scene, but whom we had forgotten, as much as though he were as **inanimate** as one of the moss-covered headstones.

'If I might be so bold,' said he again, waiting leave to speak. Jeremy bowed in deference to his white, uncovered head. And so encouraged, he went on.

'What that gentleman' (alluding to my last speech) 'has just now said, brings to my mind one who is dead and gone this many a year ago. I, may be, have not rightly understood your meaning, gentlemen, but as far as I could gather it, I think you'd both have given in to thinking poor Gilbert Dawson a hero. At any rate,' said he, heaving a long quivering sigh, 'I have reason to think him so.'

'Will you take a seat, sir, and tell us about him?' said Jeremy, standing up until the old man was seated. I confess I felt impatient at the interruption.

'It will be forty-five year come **Martinmas**,' said the Sexton, sitting down on a grassy mound at our feet, 'since I finished my 'prenticeship, and settled down at Lindal. You can see Lindal, sir, at evenings and mornings across the bay; a little to the right of Grange; at least, I used to see it, many a time and oft, afore my sight grew so dark: and I have spent many a quarter of an hour a-gazing at it far away, and thinking of the days I lived there, till the tears came so thick to my eyes, I could gaze no longer. I shall never look upon it again, either far-off or near, but you may see it, both ways, and a terrible bonny spot it is. In my young days, when I went to settle there, it was full of as wild a set of young fellows as ever were clapped eyes on; all for fighting, poaching, quarrelling, and such like work. I were startled myself when I first found what a set I were among, but soon I began to fall into their ways, and I ended by being as rough a chap as any on 'em. I'd been there a matter of two year, and were reckoned by most the cock of the village, when Gilbert Dawson, as I was speaking of, came to Lindal. He were about as strapping a chap as I was (I used to be six feet high, though now I'm so shrunk and doubled up), and, as we were like in the same trade (both used to prepare **osiers** and wood for the Liverpool **coopers**, who get a deal of stuff from the copses round the bay, sir) we were thrown together, and took mightily to each other. I put my best leg foremost to be equal with Gilbert, for I'd had some schooling, though since I'd been at Lindal I'd lost a good part of what I'd learnt; and I kept my rough ways out of sight for a time, I felt so ashamed of his getting to know them. But that did not last long. I began to think he fancied a girl I dearly loved, but who had always held off from me. Eh! but she was a pretty one in those days! There's none like her, now. I think I see her going along the road with her dancing tread, and shaking back her long yellow curls, to give me or any other young fellow a saucy word; no wonder Gilbert was taken with her, for all he was grave, and she so merry and light. But I began to think she liked him again; and then my blood was all afire. I got to hate him for everything he did. **Afore-time** I had stood

---

inanimate: lifeless
Martinmas: feast of St Martin, 11th November
osiers: strips of willow
coopers: barrel-makers
afore-time: previously

by, admiring to see him, how he leapt, and what a **quoiter** and cricketer he was. And now I ground my teeth with hatred whene'er he did a thing which caught Letty's eye. I could read it in her look that she liked him, for all she held herself just as high with him as with all the rest. Lord God forgive me! how I hated that man.'

He spoke as if the hatred were a thing of yesterday, so clear within his memory were shown the actions and feelings of his youth. And then he dropped his voice, and said:

'Well! I began to look out to pick a quarrel with him, for my blood was up to fight him. If I beat him (and I were a rare boxer in those days), I thought Letty would cool towards him. So one evening at quoits (I'm sure I don't know how or why, but large doings grow out of small words) I fell out with him, and challenged him to fight. I could see he were very wroth by his colour coming and going – and, as I said before, he were a fine active young fellow. But all at once he drew in, and said he would not fight. Such a yell as the Lindal lads, who were watching us, set up! I hear it yet. I could na' help but feel sorry for him, to be so scorned, and I thought he'd not rightly taken my meaning, and I'd give him another chance; so I said it again, and dared him, as plain as words could speak, to fight out the quarrel. He told me then, he had no quarrel against me; that he might have said something to put me up; he did not know that he had, but that if he had, he asked pardon; but that he would not fight no-how.

'I was so full of scorn at his cowardliness, that I was vexed I'd given him the second chance, and I joined in the yell that was set up, twice as bad as before. He stood it out, his teeth set, and looking very white, and when we were silent for want of breath, he said out loud, but in a hoarse voice, quite different from his own – '"I cannot fight, because I think it is wrong to quarrel, and use violence."

'Then he turned to go away; I were so beside myself with scorn and hate, that I called out –

'"Tell truth, lad, at least; if thou dare not fight, dunnot go and tell a lie about it. Mother's moppet is afraid of a black eye, pretty dear. It shannot be hurt, but it munnot tell lies."

'Well, they laughed, but I could not laugh. It seemed such a thing for a stout young chap to be a coward, and afraid!

'Before the sun had set, it was talked of all over Lindal, how I had challenged Gilbert to fight, and how he'd denied me; and the folks stood at their doors, and looked at him going up the hill to his home, as if he'd been a monkey or a foreigner, – but no one wished him good e'en. Such a thing as refusing to fight had never been heard of afore at Lindal. Next day, however, they had found voice. The men muttered the word "coward" in his hearing, and kept aloof; the women tittered as he passed, and the little impudent lads and lasses shouted out, "How long is it sin' thou turned **quaker**?" "Good-by, Jonathan **Broad-brim**," and such like jests.

'That evening I met him, with Letty by his side, coming up from the shore. She was almost crying as I came upon them at the turn of the lane; and looking

---

quoiter: quoits, a game involving throwing hoops over targets

quaker: a person who believes in peace, religious denomination

Broad-brim: type of hat associated with the Quakers

up in his face, as if begging him something. And so she
was, she told me it after. For she did really like him;
and could not abide to hear him scorned by every one
for being a coward; and she, coy as she was, all but
told him that very night that she loved him, and
begged him not to disgrace himself, but fight me as I'd
dared him to. When he still stuck to it he could not, for
that it was wrong, she was so vexed and mad-like at the
way she'd spoken, and the feelings she'd let out to coax
him, that she said more stinging things about his being
a coward than all the rest put together (according to
what she told me, sir, afterwards), and ended by saying
she'd never speak to him again, as long as she lived; –
she did once again though, – her blessing was the last
human speech that reached his ear in his wild death
struggle.

'But much happened afore that time. From the day
I met them walking, Letty turned towards me; I could
see a part of it was to spite Gilbert, for she'd be twice
as kind when he was near, or likely to hear of it; but
by-and-by she got to like me for my own sake, and it
was all settled for our marriage. Gilbert kept aloof
from every one, and fell into a sad, careless way. His
very gait was changed; his step used to be brisk and
sounding, and now his foot lingered heavily on the
ground. I used to try and daunt him with my eye, but
he would always meet my look in a steady, quiet way,
for all so much about him was altered; the lads would
not play with him; and as soon as he found he was to
be slighted by them whenever he came to quoiting or
cricket, he just left off coming.

'The old clerk was the only one he kept company
with; or perhaps, rightly to speak, the only one who
would keep company with him. They got so thick at
last, that old Jonas would say, Gilbert had gospel on

his side, and did no more than gospel told him to do; but we none of us gave much credit to what he said, more by token our vicar had a brother, a colonel in the army; and as we **threeped** it many a time to Jonas, would he set himself up to know the gospel better than the vicar? that would be putting the cart afore the horse, like the **French radicals**. And if the vicar had thought quarrelling and fighting wicked, and again the Bible, would he have made so much work about all the victories, that were as plenty as blackberries at that time of day, and kept the little bell of Lindal church for ever ringing; or would he have thought so much of "my brother the colonel," as he was always talking on?

'After I was married to Letty I left off hating Gilbert. I even kind of pitied him – he was so scorned and slighted; and for all he'd a bold look about him, as if he were not ashamed, he seemed pining and shrunk. It's a wearying thing to be kept at arm's length by one's kind; and so Gilbert found it, poor fellow. The little children took to him, though; they'd be round about him like a swarm of bees – them as was too young to know what a coward was, and only felt that he was ever ready to love and to help them, and was never loud or cross, however naughty they might be. After a while we had our little one too; such a blessed darling she was, and dearly did we love her; Letty in especial, who seemed to get all the thought I used to think sometimes she wanted, after she had her baby to care for.

---

threeped: suggested

French radicals: people who were challenging the old laws of France

'All my kin lived on this side the bay, up above Kellet. Jane (that's her that lies buried near yon white rose-tree) was to be married, and nought would serve her but that Letty and I must come to the wedding; for all my sisters loved Letty, she had such winning ways with her. Letty did not like to leave her baby, nor yet did I want her to take it: so, after a talk, we fixed to leave it with Letty's mother for the afternoon. I could see her heart ached a bit, for she'd never left it till then, and she seemed to fear all manner of evil, even to the **French coming and taking it away**. Well! we borrowed a **shandry**, and harnessed my old grey mare, as I used in th' cart, and set off as grand as King George across the Sands about three o'clock, for you see it were high water about twelve, and we'd to go and come back same tide, as Letty could not leave her baby for long. It were a merry afternoon, were that; last time I ever saw Letty laugh heartily; and for that matter, last time I ever laughed downright hearty myself. The latest crossing time fell about nine o'clock, and we were late at starting. Clocks were wrong; and we'd a piece of work chasing a pig father had given Letty to take home; we bagged him at last, and he screeched and screeched in the back part o' th' shandry, and we laughed and they laughed; and in the midst of all the merriment the sun set, and that sober'd us a bit, for then we knew what time it was. I whipped the old mare, but she was a deal **beener** than she was in the morning, and would neither go quick up nor down the brows, and they're not a few 'twixt Kellet and the shore. On the sands it were worse. They were very heavy, for the **fresh** had come down after the rains we'd had. Lord! how I did whip the poor mare, to make the most of the red light as yet lasted. You, maybe, don't know the Sands, gentlemen. From

Bolton side, where we started from, it is better than six mile to Cart-lane, and two channels to cross, let alone holes and quicksands. At the second channel from us the guide waits, all during crossing time from sunrise to sunset; – but for the three hours on each side high water he's not there, in course. He stays after sunset if he's forespoken, not else. So now you know where we were that awful night. For we'd crossed the first channel about two mile, and it were growing darker and darker above and around us, all but one red line of light above the hills, when we came to a hollow (for all the Sands look so flat, there's many a hollow in them where you lose all sight of the shore). We were longer that we should ha' been in crossing the hollow, the sand was so **quick**; and when we came up again, there, again the blackness, was the white line of the rushing tide coming up the bay! It looked not a mile from us; and when the wind blows up the bay, it comes swifter than a galloping horse. "Lord help us!" said I; and then I were sorry I'd spoken, to frighten Letty, but the words were crushed out of my heart by the terror. I felt her shiver up by my side, and clutch my coat. And as if the pig (as had screeched himself hoarse some time ago) had found out the danger we were all in, he took to squealing again, enough to bewilder any man. I cursed him between my teeth for his noise; and yet it was God's answer to my prayer, blind sinner as I was.

French coming and taking it away: a French invasion
   was feared

shandry: trap

beener: more tired

fresh: river water

quick: quick-sand, pulling under

Ay! you may smile, sir, but God can work through many a scornful thing, if need be.

'By this time the mare were all in a lather, and trembling and panting, as if in mortal fright; for though we were on the last bank afore the second channel, the water was gathering up her legs; and she so tired out! When we came close to the channel she stood still, and not all my flogging could get her to stir; she fairly groaned aloud, and shook in a terrible quaking way. Till now Letty had not spoken; only held my coat tightly. I heard her say something, and bent down my head.

'"I think, John – I think – I shall never see baby again!"

'And then she sent up such a cry – so loud and shrill, and pitiful! It fairly maddened me. I pulled out my knife to spur on the old mare, that it might end one way or the other, for the water was stealing sullenly up to the very axle tree, let alone the white waves that knew no mercy in their steady advance. That one quarter of an hour, sir, seemed as long as all my life since. Thoughts, and fancies, and dreams, and memory, ran into each other. The mist, the heavy mist, that was like a ghastly curtain, shutting us in for death, seemed to bring with it the scents of the flowers that grew around our own threshold; – it might be, for it was falling on them like blessed dew, though to us it was a shroud. Letty told me after, she heard her baby crying for her, above the gurgling of the rising waters, as plain as ever she heard anything; but the sea-birds were **skirling**, and the pig shrieking; I never caught it; it was miles away, at any rate.

'Just as I'd gotten my knife out, another sound was close upon us, blending with the gurgle of the near waters, and the roar of the distant (not so distant though); we could hardly see, but we thought we saw something black against the deep lead colour of wave, and mist, and sky. It neared, and neared: with slow, steady motion, it came across the channel right to where we were.

'O God! it was Gilbert Dawson on his strong bay horse.

'Few words did we speak, and little time had we to say them in. I had no knowledge at that moment of past or future – only of one present thought – how to save Letty, and, if I could, myself. I only remembered afterwards that Gilbert said he had been guided by an animal's shriek of terror; I only heard when all was over, that he had been uneasy about our return, because of the depth of fresh, and had borrowed a **pillion**, and saddled his horse early in the evening, and ridden down to Cart-lane to watch for us. If all had gone well, we should ne'er have heard of it. As it was, old Jonas told it, the tears down-dropping from his withered cheeks.

'We fastened his horse to the shandry. We lifted Letty to the pillion. The waters rose every instant with sullen sound. They were all but in the shandry. Letty clung to the pillion handles, but drooped her head as if she had yet no hope of life. Swifter than thought (and yet he might have had time for thought and for temptation, sir: – if he had ridden off with Letty, he would have been saved not me), Gilbert was in the shandry by my side.

'"Quick!" said he, clear and firm. "You must ride before her, and keep her up. The horse can swim. By

---

skirling: shrieking
pillion: woman's seat behind a saddle

Help arrived on a strong bay horse

God's mercy I will follow. I can cut the traces, and if the mare is not hampered with the shandry, she'll carry me safely through. At any rate, you are a husband and a father. No one cares for me."

'Do not hate me, gentlemen. I often wish that night was a dream. It has haunted my sleep ever since like a dream, and yet it was no dream. I took his place on the saddle, and put Letty's arms around me, and felt her head rest on my shoulder. I trust in God I spoke some word of thanks; but I can't remember. I only recollect Letty raising her head, and calling out, –

'"God bless you, Gilbert Dawson, for saving my baby from being an orphan this night." And then she fell against me, as if unconscious.

'I bore her through; or, rather, the strong horse swam bravely through the gathering waves. We were dripping wet when we reached the banks in-shore; but we could have but one thought – where was Gilbert? Thick mists and heaving waters compassed us round. Where was he? We shouted. Letty, faint as she was, raised her voice and shouted, clear and shrill. No answer came, the sea boomed on with ceaseless sullen beat. I rode to the guide's house. He was a-bed, and would not get up, though I offered him more than I was worth. Perhaps he knew it, the cursed old villain! At any rate I'd have paid it if I'd toiled my life long. He said I might take his horn and welcome. I did, and blew such a blast through the still, black night, the echoes came back upon the heavy air: but no human voice or sound was heard; that wild blast could not awaken the dead.

'I took Letty home to her baby, over whom she wept the live-long night. I rode back to the shore about Cart-lane; and to and fro, with weary march, did I pace along the brink of the waters, now and then shouting out into the silence a vain cry for Gilbert. The waters went back and left no trace. Two days afterwards he was washed ashore near Flukeborough. The shandry and poor old mare were found half-buried in a heap of sand by Arnside Knot. As far as we could guess, he had dropped his knife while trying to cut the traces, and so had lost all chance of life. Any rate, the knife was found in a cleft of the shaft.

'His friends came over from Garstang to his funeral. I wanted to go chief mourner, but it was not my right, and I might not; though I've never done mourning him to this day. When his sister packed up his things, I begged hard for something that had been his. She would give me none of his clothes (she was a right-down having woman), as she had boys of her own, who might grow up into them. But she threw me his Bible, as she said they'd gotten one already, and his were but a poor used-up thing. It was his, and so I cared for it. It were a black leather one, with pockets at the sides, old-fashioned-wise; and in one were a bunch of wild flowers, Letty said she could almost be sure were some she had once given him.

'There were many a text in the Gospel, marked broad with his carpenter's pencil, which more than bore him out in his refusal to fight. Of a surety, sir, there's call enough for bravery in the service of God, and to show love to man, without quarrelling and fighting.

'Thank you, gentlemen, for listening to me. Your words called up the thoughts of him, and my heart was full to speaking. But I must make up; I've to dig a grave for a little child, who is to be buried to-morrow morning, just when his playmates are trooping off to school.'

'But tell us of Letty; is she yet alive?' asked Jeremy.

The old man shook his head, and struggled against a choking sigh. After a minute's pause he said, –

'She died in less than two year after that night. She was never like the same again. She would sit thinking, on Gilbert, I guessed; but I could not blame her. We had a boy, and we named it Gilbert Dawson Knipe; he that's **stoker** on the London railway. Our girl was carried off in teething, and Letty just quietly drooped, and died in less than a six week. They were buried here; so I came to be near them, and away from Lindal, a place I could never abide after Letty was gone.'

He turned to his work, and we, having rested sufficiently, rose up, and came away.

---

stoker: one who loads coal into a steam train

The Gift of the Magi
O Henry, 1862–1910

O Henry was an American writer who was brilliant at creating short stories with a surprise at the end. He wrote over six hundred short stories, and found it very rewarding to give the unsuspecting reader a final twist in the tale.

In the following story Della and Jim are a young couple who are living on the breadline. When Christmas comes they want to buy each other a present that shows how much they value each other, but neither can afford it. Then each of them thinks of a special surprise . . .

One dollar and eighty-seven cents. That was all. And sixty cents of it was in pennies. Pennies saved one and two at a time by bulldozing the grocer and the vegetable man and the butcher until one's cheeks burned with the silent **imputation of parsimony** that such close dealing implied. Three times Della counted it. One dollar and eighty-seven cents. And the next day would be Christmas.

There was clearly nothing to do but flop down on the shabby little couch and howl. So Della did it. Which **instigates the moral reflection** that life is made up of sobs, sniffles, and smiles, with sniffles predominating.

Whilst the mistress of the home is gradually subsiding from the first stage to the second, take a look at the home. A furnished flat at eight dollars per week. It did not exactly beggar description, but it certainly had that word on the lookout for the **mendicancy** squad.

In the **vestibule** below was a letter-box into which no letter would go, and an electric button from which no mortal finger could coax a ring. Also appertaining thereunto was a card bearing the name 'Mr James Dillingham Young.'

The 'Dillingham' had been flung to the breeze during a former period of prosperity when its possessor was being paid thirty dollars per week. Now, when the income was shrunk to twenty dollars, the letters of 'Dillingham' looked blurred, as though they were thinking seriously of contracting to a modest and unassuming D. But, whenever Mr James Dillingham Young came home and reached his flat above he was called 'Jim' and greatly hugged by Mrs James Dillingham Young, already introduced to you as Della. Which is all very good.

Della finished her cry and attended to her cheeks with a powder puff. She stood by the window and looked out dully at a grey cat walking a grey fence in a grey back yard. Tomorrow would be Christmas Day, and she had only $1.87 with which to buy Jim a present. She had been saving every penny she could for months, with this result. Twenty dollars a week doesn't go far. Expenses had been greater than she had calculated. They always are. Only $1.87 to buy a present for Jim. Her Jim. Many a happy hour she had spent planning for something nice for him. Something fine and rare and sterling – something just a little bit near to being worthy of the honour of being owned by Jim.

---

imputation of parsimony: admission of poverty
instigates the moral reflection: prompts the thought
mendicancy: beggary
vestibule: hallway

Della makes a costly decision

There was a **pier glass** between the windows of the room. Perhaps you have seen a pier glass in an eight-dollar flat. A very thin and very agile person may, by observing his reflection in a rapid sequence of longitudinal strips, obtain a fairly accurate conception of his looks. Della, being slender, had mastered the art.

Suddenly she whirled from the window and stood before the glass. Her eyes were shining brilliantly, but her face had lost its colour within twenty seconds. Rapidly she pulled down her hair and let it fall to its full length.

Now, there were two possessions of the James Dillingham Youngs in which they both took a mighty pride. One was Jim's gold watch that had been his father's and his grandfather's. The other was Della's hair. Had the **Queen of Sheba** lived in the flat across the airshaft, Della would have let her hair hang out the window some day to dry just to **depreciate** Her Majesty's jewels and gifts. Had **King Solomon** been the janitor, with all his treasures piled up in the basement, Jim would have pulled out his watch every time he passed, just to see him pluck at his beard from envy.

So now Della's beautiful hair fell about her, rippling and shining like a cascade of brown water. She did it up again nervously and quickly. Once she faltered for a minute while a tear splashed on the worn red carpet.

On went her old brown jacket; on went her old brown hat. With a whirl of skirts and with the brilliant

---

pier glass: long, thin mirror
Queen of Sheba: beautiful queen of ancient Arabia
depreciate: lower in value
King Solomon: king famous for his riches

O Henry

sparkle still in her eyes, she fluttered out the door and down the stairs to the street.

Where she stopped the sign read: 'Mme. Sofronie. Hair Goods of All Kinds.' One flight up Della ran, and collected herself, panting. Madame, large, too white, chilly, hardly looked the 'Sofronie.'

'Will you buy my hair?' asked Della.

'I buy hair,' said Madame. 'Take yer hat off and let's have a sight at the looks of it.'

Down rippled the brown cascade.

'Twenty dollars,' said Madame, lifting the mass with a practised hand.

'Give it to me quick,' said Della.

Oh, and the next two hours tripped on rosy wings. Forget the **hashed metaphor**. She was ransacking the stores for Jim's present.

She found it at last. It surely had been made for Jim and no one else. There was no other like it in any of the stores, and she had turned all of them inside out. It was a platinum watch-chain, simple and chaste in design, properly proclaiming its value by substance alone and not by **meretricious ornamentation** – as all good things should do. It was even worthy of The Watch. As soon as she saw it she knew that it must be Jim's. It was like him. Quietness and value – the description applied to both. Twenty-one dollars they took from her for it, and she hurried home with the eighty-seven cents. With that chain on his watch Jim might be properly anxious about the time in any company. Grand as the watch was, he sometimes looked at it on the sly on account of the shabby old leather strap that he used in place of a proper gold chain.

When Della reached home her intoxication gave way a little to **prudence** and reason. She got out her curling-irons and lighted the gas and went to work repairing the ravages made by generosity added to love. Which is always a tremendous task, dear friends – a mammoth task.

Within forty minutes her head was covered with tiny close-lying curls that made her look wonderfully like a truant schoolboy. She looked at her reflection in the mirror long, carefully, and critically.

'If Jim doesn't kill me,' she said to herself, 'before he takes a second look at me, he'll say I look like a Coney Island chorus girl. But what could I do – oh! what could I do with a dollar and eighty-seven cents?'

At seven o'clock the coffee was made and the frying-pan was on the back of the stove, hot and ready to cook the chops.

Jim was never late. Della doubled the watch chain in her hand and sat on the corner of the table near the door that he always entered. Then she heard his step on the stair away down on the first flight, and she turned white for just a moment. She had a habit of saying little silent prayers about the simplest everyday things, and now she whispered: 'Please, God, make him think I am still pretty.'

The door opened and Jim stepped in and closed it. He looked thin and very serious. Poor fellow, he was only twenty-two – and had to be burdened with a family! He needed a new overcoat and he was without gloves.

Jim stepped inside the door, as immovable as a setter at the scent of **quail**. His eyes were fixed upon Della,

---

hashed metaphor: muddled comparison
meretricious ornamentation: flashy decoration
prudence: caution
quail: small bird which is hunted and eaten

and there was an expression in them that she could not read, and it terrified her. It was not anger, nor surprise, nor disapproval, nor horror, nor any of the sentiments that she had been prepared for. He simply stared at her fixedly with that peculiar expression on his face.

Della wriggled off the table and went for him.

'Jim, darling,' she cried, 'don't look at me that way. I had my hair cut off and sold it because I couldn't have lived through Christmas without giving you a present. It'll grow out again – you won't mind, will you? I just had to do it. My hair grows awfully fast. Say "Merry Christmas!" Jim, and let's be happy. You don't know what a nice – what a beautiful, nice gift I've got for you.'

'You've cut off your hair?' asked Jim, laboriously, as if he had not arrived at that patent fact yet even after the hardest mental labour.

'Cut it off and sold it,' said Della. 'Don't you like me just as well, anyhow? I'm me without my hair, ain't I?'

Jim looked about the room curiously.

'You say your hair is gone?' he said, with an air almost of idiocy.

'You needn't look for it,' said Della. 'It's sold, I tell you – sold and gone, too. It's Christmas Eve, boy. Be good to me, for it went for you. Maybe the hairs of my head were numbered,' she went on with a sudden serious sweetness, 'but nobody could ever count my love for you. Shall I put the chops on, Jim?'

Out of his trance Jim seemed to quickly wake. He enfolded his Della. For ten seconds let us regard with discreet scrutiny some inconsequential object in the other direction. Eight dollars a week or a million a year – what is the difference? A mathematician or a wit would give you the wrong answer. The Magi brought valuable gifts, but that was not among them. This dark assertion will be illuminated later on.

Jim drew a package from his overcoat pocket and threw it upon the table.

'Don't make any mistake, Dell,' he said, 'about me. I don't think there's anything in the way of a haircut or a shave or a shampoo that could make me like my girl any less. But if you'll unwrap that package you may see why you had me going awhile at first.'

White fingers and nimble tore at the string and paper. And then an ecstatic scream of joy; and then, alas! a quick feminine change to hysterical tears and wails, **necessitating the immediate employment** of all the comforting powers of the lord of the flat.

For there lay The Combs – the set of combs that Della had worshipped for long in a Broadway window. Beautiful combs, pure tortoise shell, with jewelled rims – just the shade to wear in the beautiful vanished hair. They were expensive combs, she knew, and her heart had simply craved and yearned over them without the least hope of possession. And now they were hers, but the tresses that should have adorned the coveted adornments were gone.

But she hugged them to her bosom, and at length she was able to look up with dim eyes and a smile and say: 'My hair grows so fast, Jim!'

And then Della leaped up like a little singed cat and cried, 'Oh, oh!'

Jim had not yet seen his beautiful present. She held it out to him eagerly upon her open palm. The dull precious metal seemed to flash with a reflection of her ardent spirit.

'Isn't it a dandy, Jim? I hunted all over town to find

---

necessitating the immediate employment: needing fast action

it. You'll have to look at the time a hundred times a day
now. Give me your watch. I want to see how it looks on
it.'

Instead of obeying, Jim tumbled down on the couch
and put his hands under the back of his head and
smiled.

'Dell,' said he, 'let's put our Christmas presents
away and keep 'em awhile. They're too nice to use just
at present. I sold the watch to get the money to buy
your combs. And now suppose you put the chops on.'

The Magi, as you know, were wise men – wonderfully wise men – who brought gifts to the Babe in the
manger. They invented the art of giving Christmas
presents. Being wise, their gifts were no doubt wise
ones, possibly bearing the privilege of exchange in case
of duplication. And here I have lamely related to you
the uneventful chronicle of two foolish children in a
flat who most unwisely sacrificed for each other the
greatest treasures of their house. But in a last word to
the wise of these days let it be said that of all who give
gifts these two were the wisest. Of all who give and
receive gifts, such as they are the wisest. Everywhere
they are the wisest. They are the Magi.

The Parvenue

Mary Shelley, 1796–1851

Mary Shelley is probably best known as the author of Frankenstein *but she was a colourful character in herself, and led an extraordinary, and at the time shocking, life. She eloped with Percy Bysshe Shelley and married him after his wife's suicide. They travelled around Europe a great deal, often with other writers including Lord Byron who was described as 'mad, bad and dangerous to know'. It was Byron's idea of a competition to write a horror story which prompted Mary to write* Frankenstein. *Two of her children and her unfaithful husband died before her and she was often alone and dejected.*

The Parvenue *is about a young girl who marries a man who is her social superior at a time when it was usual to marry someone of one's own 'social class'. Surprisingly, the marriage suits everyone at first, but then the complications begin . . .*

Why do I write my **melancholy** story? Is it as a lesson, to prevent any other from wishing to rise to rank superior to that in which they are born? No, miserable as I am, others might have been happy, I doubt not, in my position: the **chalice** has been poisoned for me alone! Am I evil-minded – am I

---

parvenue: an upstart
melancholy: sad
chalice: cup

---

wicked? What have been my errors, that I am now an
outcast and wretched? I will tell my story – let others
judge me; my mind is bewildered, I cannot judge
myself.

My father was land steward to a wealthy nobleman.
He married young, and had several children. He then
lost his wife, and remained fifteen years a widower,
when he married again a young girl, the daughter of a
clergyman who died leaving numerous offspring in
extreme poverty. My maternal grandfather had been a
man of sensibility and genius; my mother inherited
many of his **endowments**. She was an angel on earth;
all her works were charity, all her thoughts were love.

Within a year after her marriage, she gave birth to
twins – I and my sister; soon after she fell into
ill-health, and from that time was always weakly. She
could endure no fatigue, and seldom moved from her
chair. I see her now; – her white, delicate hands
employed in needlework, her soft, love-lighted eyes
fixed on me. I was still a child when my father fell into
trouble, and we removed from the part of the country
where we had hitherto lived, and went to a distant
village, where we rented a cottage, with a little land
adjoining. We were poor, and all the family assisted
each other. My elder half-sisters were strong, industrious, rustic young women, and submitted to a life of
labour with great cheerfulness. My father held the
plough, my half-brothers worked in the barns; all was
toil, yet all seemed enjoyment.

How happy my childhood was! Hand in hand with
my dear twin-sister, I plucked the spring flowers in the
hedges, turned the hay in the summer meadows, shook
the apples from the trees in the autumn, and at all
seasons, gambolled in delicious liberty beneath the
free air of heaven; or at my mother's feet, caressed by

her, I was taught the sweetest lessons of charity and love. My elder sisters were kind; we were all linked by strong affection. The delicate, fragile existence of my mother gave an interest to our monotony, while her virtues and her refinement threw a grace over our homely household.

I and my sister did not seem twins, we were so unlike. She was robust, chubby, full of life and spirits; I, tall, slim, fair, and even pale. I loved to play with her, but soon grew tired, and then I crept to my mother's side, and she sang me to sleep, and nursed me in her bosom, and looked on me with her own angelic smile. She took pains to instruct me, not in accomplishments, but in all real knowledge. She unfolded to me the wonders of the visible creation, and to each tale of bird and beast, of fiery mountain or vast river, was **appended** some moral, derived from her warm heart and ardent imagination. Above all, she impressed upon me the **precepts** of the gospel, charity to every fellow-creature, the brotherhood of mankind, the rights that every **sentient** creature possesses to our service. I was her **almoner**; for, poor as she was, she was the **benefactress** of those who were poorer. Being delicate, I helped her in her task of needlework, while my sister aided the rest in their household or rustic labours.

---

endowments: qualities
appended: attached
precepts: teachings
sentient: capable of feeling
almoner: one who distributes help to the poor
benefactress: one who donates help to the poor

I felt myself seized upon and borne away

When I was seventeen, a miserable accident happened. A hayrick caught fire; it communicated to our outhouses, and at last to the cottage. We were roused from our beds at midnight, and escaped barely with our lives. My father bore out my mother in his arms, and then tried to save a portion of his property. The roof of the cottage fell in on him. He was dug out after an hour, scorched, maimed, crippled for life.

We were all saved, but by a miracle only was I preserved. I and my sister were awoke by cries of fire. The cottage was already enveloped in flames. Susan, with her accustomed **intrepidity**, rushed through the flames, and escaped; I thought only of my mother, and hurried to her room. The fire raged around me; it encircled – hemmed me in. I believed that I must die, when suddenly I felt myself seized upon and borne away. I looked on my preserver – it was Lord Reginald Desborough.

For many Sundays past, when at church, I knew that Lord Reginald's eyes were fixed on me. He had met me and Susan in our walks; he had called at our cottage. There was fascination in his eye, in his soft voice and earnest gaze, and my heart throbbed with gladness, as I thought that he surely loved me. To have been saved by him was to make the **boon** of life doubly precious.

There is to me much obscurity in this part of my story. Lord Reginald loved me, it is true; why he loved me, so far as to forget pride of rank and ambition for my sake, he who afterwards showed no tendency to disregard the prejudices and habits of rank and wealth, I cannot tell; it seems strange. He had loved me

---

intrepidity: bravery
boon: gift

before, but from the hour that he saved my life, love grew into an overpowering passion. He offered us a lodge on his estate to take refuge in; and while there, he sent us presents of **game**, and still more kindly, fruits and flowers to my mother, and came himself, especially when all were out except my mother and myself, and sat by us and conversed. Soon I learnt to expect the soft asking look of his eyes, and almost dared answer it. My mother once perceived these glances, and took an opportunity to appeal to Lord Reginald's good feelings, not to make me miserable for life, by implanting an attachment that could only be productive of unhappiness. His answer was to ask me in marriage.

I need not say that my mother gratefully consented; that my father, confined to his bed since the fire, thanked God with rapture; that my sisters were transported by delight: I was the least surprised then, though the most happy. Now, I wonder much, what could he see in me? So many girls of rank and fortune were prettier. I was an untaught, low-born, **portionless** girl. It was very strange.

Then I only thought of the happiness of marrying him, of being loved, of passing my life with him. My wedding day was fixed. Lord Reginald had neither father nor mother to interfere with his arrangements. He told no relation; he became one of our family during the interval. He saw no deficiencies in our mode of life – in my dress; he was satisfied with all; he was tender, **assiduous**, and kind, even to my elder sisters; he seemed to adore my mother, and became a brother to my sister Susan. She was in love, and asked him to intercede to gain her parents' consent for her choice. He did so; and though before, Lawrence Cooper, the carpenter of the place, had been disdained, supported by him, he was accepted. Lawrence Cooper was young, well-looking, well disposed, and fondly attached to Susan.

My wedding day came. My mother kissed me fondly, my father blessed me with pride and joy, my sisters stood round, radiant with delight. There was but one drawback to the universal happiness – that immediately on my marriage I was to go abroad.

From the church door I stepped into the carriage. Having once and again been folded in my dear mother's embrace, the wheels were in motion, and we were away. I looked out from the window; there was the dear group: my old father, white-headed and aged, in his large chair; my mother, smiling through her tears, with folded hands and upraised looks of gratitude, anticipating long years of happiness for her child; Susan and Lawrence standing side by side, unenvious of my greatness, happy in themselves; my sisters **conning** over with pride and joy the presents made to them, and the prosperity that flowed in from my husband's generosity. All looked happy, and it seemed as if I were the cause of all this happiness. We had been indeed saved from dreadful evils; ruin had ensued from the fire, and we had been sunk in adversity through that very event from which our good fortune took its rise. I felt proud and glad. I loved them all. I thought, I make them happy – they are

---

game: rabbits, duck, etc. shot by hunters

portionless: having no dowry (money paid by the bride's father to her husband's family)

assiduous: constant, attentive

conning: looking over

prosperous through me! And my heart warmed with gratitude towards my husband at the idea.

We spent two years abroad. It was rather lonely for me, who had always been surrounded, as it were, by a populous world of my own, to find myself cast upon foreigners and strangers; the habits of the different sexes in the higher ranks so separate them from each other, that, after a few months, I spent much of my time in solitude. I did not **repine**; I had been brought up to look upon the **hard visage of life**, if not unflinchingly, at least with resignation. I did not expect perfect happiness. Marriages in humble life are attended with so much care. I had none of this; my husband loved me; and though I often longed to see the dear familiar faces that thronged my childhood's home, and, above all, pined for my mother's caresses and her wise maternal lessons, yet for a time I was content to think of them, and hope for a reunion.

Still many things pained me. I had, poor myself, been brought up among the poor, and nothing, since I can remember forming an idea, so much astonished and jarred with my feelings as the thought of how the rich could spend so much on themselves, while any of their fellow-creatures were in destitution. I had none of the **patrician** charity (though such is praise-worthy), which consists in distributing thin soup and coarse flannel petticoats – a sort of instinct or sentiment of justice, the offspring of my lowly paternal hearth, and my mother's enlightened **piety**, was deeply implanted in my mind, that all had as good a right to the comforts of life as myself, or even as my husband. My charities, they were called – they seemed to me the payment of my debts to my fellow-creatures – were abundant. Lord Reginald **peremptorily checked** them; but as I had a large allowance for my own expenses, I denied myself a thousand luxuries, for the sake of feeding the hungry. Nor was it only that charity impelled me, but that I could not acquire a taste for spending money on myself – I disliked the **apparatus** of wealth. My husband called my ideas sordid, and reproved me severely, when, instead of outshining all competitors at a fête, I appeared dowdily dressed, and declared warmly that I could not, I would not, spend twenty guineas for a gown, while I could dress many sad faces in smiles, and bring much joy to many drooping hearts, by the same sum.

Was I right? I firmly believe that there is not one among the rich who will not affirm that I did wrong; that to please my husband, and do honour to his rank, was my first duty. Yet, shall I confess it? even now, rendered miserable by this fault – I cannot give it that name – I can call it a misfortune – I have wasted at the slow fire of knowing that I lost my husband's affections because I performed what I believed to be a duty.

But I am not come to that yet. It was not till my return to England that the full disaster crushed me. We had often been applied to for money by my family, and Lord Reginald had acceded to nearly all their requests. When we reached London, after two years' absence, my first wish was to see my dear mother. She was at Margate for her health. It was agreed that I

---

repine: complain

hard visage of life: difficulties of life

patrician: noble

piety: devotion

peremptorily checked: put a stop to without hesitation

apparatus: outward show

should go there alone, and pay a short visit. Before I went, Lord Reginald told me what I did not know before, that my family had often made exorbitant demands on him, with which he was resolved not to comply. He told me that he had no wish to raise my relatives from their station in society; and that, indeed, there were only two among them whom he conceived had any claims upon me – my mother and my twin-sister: that the former was incapable of any improper request, and the latter, by marrying Cooper, had fixed her own position, and could in no way be raised from the rank of her chosen husband. I agreed to much that he said. I replied that he well knew that my own taste led me to consider **mediocrity** the best and happiest situation; that I had no wish, and would never consent, to supply any extravagant demands on the part of persons, however dear to me, whose circumstances he had rendered easy.

Satisfied with my reply, we parted most affectionately, and I went on my way to Margate with a light and glad heart; and the cordial reception I received from my whole family collected together to receive me, was calculated to add to my satisfaction. The only drawback to my content was my mother's state; she was wasted to a shadow. They all talked and laughed around her, but it was evident to me that she had not long to live.

There was no room for me in the small furnished house in which they were all crowded, so I remained at the hotel. Early in the morning, before I was up, my father visited me. He begged me to intercede with my husband; that on the strength of his support he had embarked in a speculation which required a large capital; that many families would be ruined, and himself dishonoured, if a few hundreds were not advanced. I promised to do what I could, resolving to ask my mother's advice, and make her my guide. My father kissed me with an effusion of gratitude, and left me.

I cannot enter into the whole of these sad details; all my half brothers and sisters had married, and trusted to their success in life to Lord Reginald's assistance. Each evidently thought that they asked little in not demanding an equal share of my luxuries and fortune; but they were all in difficulty – all needed large assistance – all depended on me.

Lastly, my own sister Susan appealed to me – but hers was the most moderate request of all – she only wished for twenty pounds. I gave it her at once from my own purse.

As soon as I saw my mother I explained to her my difficulties. She told me that she expected this, and that it broke her heart: I must summon courage and resist these demands. That my father's imprudence had ruined him, and that he must encounter the evil he had brought on himself; that my numerous relatives were absolutely mad with the notion of what I ought to do for them. I listened with grief – I saw the torments in store for me – I felt my own weakness, and knew that I could not meet the **rapacity** of those about me with any courage or firmness. That same night my mother fell into convulsions; her life was saved with difficulty. From Susan I learned the cause of her attack. She had had a violent **altercation** with my father: she insisted that I should not be appealed to;

---

mediocrity: the average
rapacity: grasping, greed
altercation: argument

I waited with anguish for my husband's answer

while he reproached her for rendering me undutiful, and bringing ruin and disgrace on his grey hairs. When I saw my pale mother trembling, fainting, dying – when I was again and again assured that she must be my father's victim unless I yielded, what wonder that, in the agony of my distress, I wrote to my husband to implore his assistance.

Oh, what thick clouds now obscured my destiny! how do I remember, with a sort of thrilling horror, the boundless sea, white cliffs, and wide sands of Margate! The summer day that had welcomed my arrival changed to bleak wintry weather during this interval – while I waited with anguish for my husband's answer. Well do I remember the evening on which it came: the waves of the sea showed their white crests, no vessel ventured to meet the gale with any canvas except a topsail, the sky was bared clear by the wind, the sun was going down fiery red. I looked upon the troubled waters – I longed to be borne away upon them, away from care and misery. At this moment a servant followed me to the sands with my husband's answer – it contained a refusal. I dared not communicate it. The menaces of bankruptcy; the knowledge that he had instilled false hopes into so many; the fears of disgrace, rendered my father, always rough, absolutely ferocious. Life flickered in my dear mother's frame, it seemed on the point of expiring when she heard my father's step; if he came in with a smooth brow, her pale lips wreathed into her own sweet smile, and a delicate pink tinged her fallen cheeks; if he scowled, and his voice was high, every limb shivered, she turned her face to her pillow, while convulsive tears shook her frame, and threatened instant **dissolution**. My father

---

dissolution: death

sought me alone one day, as I was walking in melancholy guise upon the sands; he swore that he would not survive his disgrace. 'And do you think, Fanny,' he added, 'that your mother will survive the knowledge of my miserable end?' I saw the resolution of despair in his face as he spoke. – I asked the sum needed, the time when it must be given. – A thousand pounds in two days was all that was asked. I set off to London to implore my husband to give this sum.

No! no! I cannot step by step record my wretchedness – the money was given – I extorted it from Lord Reginald, though I saw his heart closed on me as he wrote the cheque. Worse had happened since I had left him. Susan had used the twenty pounds I gave her to reach town, to throw herself at my husband's feet, and implore his compassion. Rendered absolutely insane by the idea of having a lord for a brother-in-law, Cooper had launched into a system of extravagance, incredible as it was wicked. He was many thousands of pounds in debt, and when at last Lord Reginald wrote to refuse all further supply, the miserable man committed forgery. Two hundred pounds prevented exposure, and preserved him from an **ignominious** end. Five hundred more were advanced to send him and his wife to America, to settle there, out of the way of temptation. I parted from my dear sister – I loved her fondly; she had no part in her husband's guilt, yet she was still attached to him, and her child bound them together; they went into solitary, miserable exile. 'Ah! had we remained in virtuous poverty,' cried my broken-hearted sister, 'I had not been forced to leave my dying mother.'

The thousand pounds given to my father was but a drop of water in the ocean. Again I was appealed to; again I felt the slender thread of my mother's life depended on my getting a supply. Again, trembling and miserable, I implored the charity of my husband.

'I am content,' he said, 'to do what you ask, to do more than you ask; but remember the price you pay – either give up your parents and your family, whose rapacity and crimes deserve no mercy, or we part for ever. You shall have a proper allowance; you can maintain all your family on it if you please; but their names must never be mentioned to me again. Choose between us – you never see them more, or we part for ever.'

Did I do right – I cannot tell – misery is the result – misery frightful, endless, unredeemed. My mother was dearer to me than all the world. I did not reply – I rushed to my room, and that night, in a delirium of grief and horror, I set out for Margate – such was my reply to my husband.

Three years have passed since then; and during all this time I was grateful to Heaven for being permitted to do my duty by my mother; and though I wept over the **alienation** of my husband, I did not repent. But she, my angelic support, is no more. My father survived my mother but two months; remorse for all he had done, and made me suffer, cut short his life. His family by his first wife are gathered round me; they **importune**, they rob, they destroy me. Last week I wrote to Lord Reginald. I communicated the death of my parents; I represented that my position was altered; and that if he still cared for his unhappy wife all might be well. Yesterday his answer came. – It was

---

ignominious: shameful
alienation: separation from, loss
importune: beg

too late, he said: – I had myself torn asunder the ties that united us – they never could be knit together again.

By the same post came a letter from Susan. She is happy. Cooper, awakened to a manly sense of the duties of life, is thoroughly reformed. He is industrious and prosperous. Susan asks me to join her. I am resolved to go. Oh! my home, and recollections of my youth, where are ye now? **envenomed** by serpents' stings, I long to close my eyes on every scene I have ever viewed. Let me seek a strange land, a land where a grave will soon be opened for me. I desire to die. I am told that Lord Reginald loves another, a high-born girl; that he openly curses our union as the obstacle to his happiness. The memory of this will poison the oblivion I go to seek. He will soon be free. Soon will the hand he once so fondly took in his and made his own, which, now flung away, trembles with misery as it traces these lines, moulder in its last decay.

---

envenomed: poisoned

An Alpine Divorce
Robert Barr, 1850–1912

Robert Barr was born in Glasgow in 1850. He later moved to Canada where he taught English, and then moved on to Detroit where he worked as a journalist with the 'Free Press'. He returned to England, settling in London, and started to write fiction.

This story was written in 1887 and could easily be a modern tale, with its strong characters and wonderfully unexpected ending. Mr and Mrs Bodman take a holiday together in the Swiss Alps. But unknown to each other, they both have deadly plans . . .

In some natures there are no **half-tones**; nothing but raw primary colours. John Bodman was a man who was always at one extreme or the other. This probably would have mattered little had he not married a wife whose nature was an exact duplicate of his own.

Doubtless there exists in this world precisely the right woman for any given man to marry, and vice versa; but when you consider that a human being has the opportunity of being acquainted with only a few hundred people, and out of the few hundred that there are but a dozen or less whom he knows intimately, and, out of the dozen, one or two friends at most, it will easily be seen, when we remember the number of millions who inhabit this world, that probably since

---

half-tones: various shades of grey

---

the earth was created the right man has never yet met the right woman. The mathematical chances are all against such a meeting, and this is the reason that divorce courts exist. Marriage at best is but a **compromise**, and if two people happen to be united who are of an uncompromising nature there is trouble.

In the lives of these two young people there was no middle distance. The result was bound to be either love or hate, and in the case of Mr and Mrs Bodman it was hate of the most bitter and arrogant kind.

In some parts of the world **incompatibility of temper** is considered a just cause for obtaining a divorce, but in England no such subtle distinction is made, and so, until the wife became criminal, or the man became both criminal and cruel, these two were linked together by a bond that only death could sever. Nothing can be worse than this state of things, and the matter was only made the more hopeless by the fact that Mrs Bodman lived a blameless life, and her husband was no worse, but rather better, than the majority of men. Perhaps, however, that statement held only up to a certain point, for John Bodman had reached a state of mind in which he resolved to get rid of his wife at all hazards. If he had been a poor man he would probably have deserted her, but he was rich, and a man cannot freely leave a prospering business because his domestic life happens not to be happy.

When a man's mind dwells too much on any one subject, no one can tell just how far he will go. The mind is a delicate instrument, and even the law recognises that it is easily thrown from its balance. Bodman's friends – for he had friends – claim that his mind was unhinged; but neither his friends nor his enemies suspected the truth of the episode, which turned out to be the most important, as it was the most **ominous**, event in his life.

Whether John Bodman was sane or insane at the time he made up his mind to murder his wife will never be known, but there was certainly craftiness in the method he devised to make the crime appear the result of an accident. Nevertheless, cunning is often a quality in a mind that has gone wrong.

Mrs Bodman well knew how much her presence **afflicted** her husband, but her nature was as relentless as his, and her hatred of him was, if possible, more bitter than his hatred of her. Wherever he went she accompanied him, and perhaps the idea of murder would never have occurred to him if she had not been so persistent in forcing her presence upon him at all times and on all occasions. So, when he announced to her that he intended to spend the month of July in Switzerland, she said nothing, but made her preparations for the journey. On this occasion he did not protest, as was usual with him, and so to Switzerland this silent couple departed.

There is a hotel near the mountain-tops, which stands on a ledge over one of the great glaciers. It is a mile and a half above the level of the sea, and it stands alone, reached by a toilsome road that zigzags up the mountain for six miles. There is a wonderful view of snow-peaks and glaciers from the verandahs of this hotel, and in the neighbourhood are many picturesque walks to points more or less dangerous.

---

compromise: agreement, settlement of a middle way
incompatibility of temper: personalities which clash
ominous: evil
afflicted: upset

John Bodman knew the hotel well, and in happier days he had been **intimately acquainted** with the vicinity. Now that the thought of murder arose in his mind, a certain spot two miles distant from this inn continually haunted him. It was a point of view overlooking everything, and its extremity was protected by a low and crumbling wall. He arose one morning at four o'clock, slipped unnoticed out of the hotel, and went to this point, which was locally named the Hanging Outlook. His memory had served him well. It was exactly the spot, he said to himself. The mountain which rose up behind it was wild and **precipitous**. There were no inhabitants near to overlook the place. The distant hotel was hidden by a shoulder of rock. The mountains on the other side of the valley were too far away to make it possible for any casual tourist or native to see what was going on on the Hanging Outlook. Far down in the valley the only town in view seemed like a collection of little toy houses.

One glance over the crumbling wall at the edge was generally sufficient for a visitor of even the strongest nerves. There was a sheer drop of more than a mile straight down, and at the distant bottom were jagged rocks and stunted trees that looked, in the blue haze, like shrubbery.

'This is the spot,' said the man to himself, 'and tomorrow morning is the time.'

John Bodman had planned his crime as grimly and relentlessly, and as coolly, as ever he had concocted a deal on the Stock Exchange. There was no thought in his mind of mercy for his unconscious victim. His hatred had carried him far.

The next morning, after breakfast, he said to his wife: 'I intend to take a walk in the mountains. Do you wish to come with me?'

'Yes,' she answered briefly.

'Very well, then,' he said; 'I shall be ready at nine o'clock.'

'I shall be ready at nine o'clock,' she repeated after him.

At that hour they left the hotel together, to which he was shortly to return alone. They spoke no word to each other on their way to the Hanging Outlook. The path was practically level, skirting the mountains, for the Hanging Outlook was not much higher above the sea than the hotel.

John Bodman had formed no fixed plan for his procedure when the place was reached. He resolved to be guided by circumstances. Now and then a strange fear arose in his mind that she might cling to him and possibly drag him over the **precipice** with her. He found himself wondering whether she had any **premonition** of her fate, and one of his reasons for not speaking was the fear that a tremor in his voice might possibly arouse her suspicions. He resolved that his action should be sharp and sudden, that she might have no choice either to help herself or to drag him with her. Of her screams in that desolate region he had no fear. No one could reach the spot except from the hotel, and no one that morning had left the house, even for an expedition to the glacier – one of the easiest and most popular trips from the place.

Curiously enough, when they came within sight of the Hanging Outlook, Mrs Bodman stopped and

intimately acquainted: very familiar

precipitous: very steep

precipice: vertical or steep face of mountain etc

premonition: forewarning

Bodman sat down upon the crumbling wall

shuddered. Bodman looked at her through the narrow slits of his veiled eyes, and wondered again if she had any suspicion. No one can tell, when two people walk closely together, what unconscious communication one mind may have with another.

'What is the matter?' he asked gruffly. 'Are you tired?'

'John,' she cried, with a gasp in her voice, calling him by his Christian name for the first time in years, 'don't you think that if you had been kinder to me at first things might have been different?'

'It seems to me,' he answered, not looking at her, 'that it is rather late in the day for discussing that question.'

'I have much to regret,' she said quaveringly. 'Have you nothing?'

'No,' he answered.

'Very well,' replied his wife, with the usual hardness returning to her voice. 'I was merely giving you a chance. Remember that.'

Her husband looked at her suspiciously.

'What do you mean?' he asked, 'giving me a chance? I want no chance nor anything else from you. A man accepts nothing from one he hates. My feeling towards you is, I imagine, no secret to you. We are tied together, and you have done your best to make the **bondage insupportable**.'

'Yes,' she answered, with her eyes on the ground, 'we are tied together – we are tied together!'

She repeated these words under her breath as they walked the few remaining steps to the Outlook. Bodman sat down upon the crumbling wall. The woman dropped her **alpenstock** on the rock, and walked nervously to

---

bondage insupportable: make the marriage very unhappy
alpenstock: walking stick

and fro, clasping and unclasping her hands. Her husband caught his breath as the terrible moment drew near.

'Why do you walk about like a wild animal?' he cried. 'Come here and sit down beside me, and be still.'

She faced him with a light he had never before seen in her eyes – a light of insanity and of hatred.

'I walk like a wild animal,' she said, 'because I am one. You spoke a moment ago of your hatred of me; but you are a man, and your hatred is nothing to mine. Bad as you are, much as you wish to break the bond which ties us together, there are still things which I know you would not stoop to. I know there is no thought of murder in your heart, but there is in mine. I will show you, John Bodman, how much I hate you.'

The man nervously clutched the stone beside him, and gave a guilty start as she mentioned murder.

'Yes,' she continued, 'I have told all my friends in England that I believed you intended to murder me in Switzerland.'

'Good God!' he cried. 'How could you say such a thing?'

'I say it to show how much I hate you – how much I am prepared to give for revenge. I have warned the people at the hotel, and when we left two men followed us. The proprietor tried to persuade me not to accompany you. In a few moments those two men will come in sight of the Outlook. Tell them, if you think they will believe you, that it was an accident.'

The mad woman tore from the front of her dress shreds of lace and scattered them around.

Bodman started up to his feet, crying, 'What are you about?' But before he could move toward her she **precipitated** herself over the wall, and went shrieking and whirling down the awful **abyss**.

The next moment two men came hurriedly round the edge of the rock and found the man standing alone. Even in his bewilderment he realized that if he told the truth he would not be believed.

---

precipitated: threw headlong
abyss: deep chasm, opening in the earth

The Thieves who Couldn't Help Sneezing
Thomas Hardy, 1840–1928

Thomas Hardy was born in the country and grew up with farmers, tradesmen and landowners. When he was older he invented an area which he called 'Wessex'. He set his novels there, basing his location and characters on real people and places.

When thieves set on 14-year-old Hubert one cold Christmas Eve, they leave him tied up and set off for their next burglary. But they haven't counted on the cunning and courage of Hubert . . .

Many years ago, when oak trees now past their prime were about as large as elderly gentlemen's walking-sticks, there lived in Wessex a **yeoman's** son, whose name was Hubert. He was about fourteen years of age, and was as remarkable for his **candour** and lightness of heart as for his physical courage, of which, indeed, he was a little vain.

One cold Christmas Eve his father, having no other help at hand, sent him on an important errand to a small town several miles from home. He travelled on horseback, and was detained by the business till a late hour of the evening. At last, however, it was completed; he returned to the inn, the horse was saddled, and he started on his way. His journey homeward lay through the Vale of Blackmore, a fertile but somewhat lonely district, with heavy clay roads and crooked lanes. In those days, too, a great part of it was thickly wooded.

It must have been about nine o'clock when, riding along amid the overhanging trees upon his stout-legged cob, Jerry, and singing a Christmas carol, to be in harmony with the season, Hubert fancied that he heard a noise among the boughs. This recalled to his mind that the spot he was traversing bore an evil name. Men had been **waylaid** there. He looked at Jerry, and wished he had been of any other colour than light grey; for on this account the docile animal's form was visible even here in the dense shade. 'What do I care?' he said aloud, after a few minutes of reflection. 'Jerry's legs are too nimble to allow any highwayman to come near me.'

'Ha! Ha! indeed,' was said in a deep voice; and the next moment a man darted from the thicket on his right hand, another man from the thicket on his left hand, and another from a tree-trunk a few yards ahead. Hubert's bridle was seized, he was pulled from his horse, and although he struck out with all his might, as a brave boy would naturally do, he was overpowered. His arms were tied behind him, his legs bound tightly together, and he was thrown into a ditch. The robbers, whose faces he could now dimly perceive to be artificially blackened, at once departed, leading off the horse.

As soon as Hubert had a little recovered himself, he found that by great exertion he was able to **extricate** his legs from the cord; but, in spite of every endeavour, his arms remained bound as fast as before. All,

---

yeoman: farmer
candour: openness, honesty
waylaid: robbed
extricate: free

Hubert struggled desperately with his attackers

therefore, that he could do was to rise to his feet and proceed on his way with his arms behind him, and trust to chance for getting them unfastened. He knew that it would be impossible to reach home on foot that night, and in such a condition; but he walked on. Owing to the confusion which this attack caused in his brain, he lost his way, and would have been inclined to lie down and rest till morning among the dead leaves had he not known the danger of sleeping without wrappers in a frost so severe. So he wandered farther onwards, his arms wrung and numbed by the cord which **pinioned** him, and his heart aching for the loss of poor Jerry, who never had been known to kick, or bite, or show a single vicious habit. He was not a little glad when he discerned through the trees a distant light. Towards this he made his way, and presently found himself in front of a large mansion with flanking wings, gables, and towers, the battlements and chimneys showing their shapes against the stars.

All was silent; but the door stood wide open, it being from this door that the light shone which had attracted him. On entering he found himself in a vast apartment arranged as a dining-hall, and brilliantly illuminated. The walls were covered with a great deal of dark wainscoting, formed into moulded panels, carvings, closet-doors, and the usual fittings of a house of that kind. But what drew his attention most was the large table in the midst of the hall, upon which was spread a sumptuous supper, as yet untouched. Chairs were placed around, and it appeared as if something had occurred to interrupt the meal just at the time when all were ready to begin.

---

pinioned: bound

Even had Hubert been so inclined, he could not have eaten in his helpless state, unless by dipping his mouth into the dishes, like a pig or cow. He wished first to obtain assistance; and was about to penetrate farther into the house for that purpose when he heard hasty footsteps in the porch and the words, 'Be quick!' uttered in the deep voice which had reached him when he was dragged from the horse. There was only just time for him to dart under the table before three men entered the dining-hall. Peeping from beneath the hanging edges of the tablecloth, he perceived that their faces, too, were blackened, which at once removed any doubts he may have felt that these were the same thieves.

'Now, then,' said the first – the man with the deep voice – 'let us hide ourselves. They will all be back again in a minute. That was a good trick to get them out of the house – eh?'

'Yes. You well imitated the cries of a man in distress,' said the second.

'Excellently,' said the third.

'But they will soon find out that it was a false alarm. Come, where shall we hide? It must be some place we can stay in for two or three hours, till all are in bed and asleep. Ah! I have it. Come this way! I have learnt that the farther cupboard is not opened once in a twelve-month; it will serve our purpose exactly.'

The speaker advanced into a corridor which led from the hall. Creeping a little farther forward, Hubert could discern that the cupboard stood at the end, facing the dining-hall. The thieves entered it, and closed the door. Hardly breathing, Hubert glided forward, to learn a little more of their intention, if possible; and, coming close, he could hear the robbers whispering about the different rooms where the jewels, plate, and other valuables of the house were kept, which they plainly meant to steal.

They had not been long in hiding when a gay chattering of ladies and gentlemen was **audible** on the terrace without. Hubert felt that it would not do to be caught prowling about the house, unless he wished to be taken for a robber himself, and stood in a dark corner of the porch, where he could see everything without being himself seen. In a moment or two a whole troop of personages came gliding past him into the house. There were an elderly gentleman and lady, eight or nine young ladies, as many young men, besides half a dozen menservants and maids. The mansion had apparently been quite emptied of its occupants.

'Now, children and young people, we will resume our meal,' said the old gentleman. 'What the noise could have been I cannot understand. I never felt so certain in my life that there was a person being murdered outside my door.'

Then the ladies began saying how frightened they had been, and how they had expected an adventure, and how it had ended in nothing after all.

'Wait a while,' said Hubert to himself. 'You'll have adventure enough by and by, ladies.'

It appeared that the young men and women were married sons and daughters of the old couple, who had come that day to spend Christmas with their parents.

The door was then closed, Hubert being left outside in the porch. He thought this a proper moment for asking their assistance; and, since he was unable to knock with his hands, began boldly to kick the door.

---

audible: able to be heard

'Hallo! What disturbance are you making here?' said a footman who opened it; and, seizing Hubert by the shoulder, he pulled him into the dining-hall. 'Here's a strange boy I have found making a noise in the porch, Sir Simon.'

Everybody turned.

'Bring him forward,' said Sir Simon, the old gentleman before mentioned. 'What were you doing there, my boy?'

'Why, his arms are tied!' said one of the ladies.

'Poor fellow!' said another.

Hubert at once began to explain that he had been waylaid on his journey home, robbed of his horse, and mercilessly left in this condition by the thieves.

'Only to think of it!' exclaimed Sir Simon.

'That's a likely story,' said one of the gentlemen-guests, incredulously.

'Doubtful, hey?' asked Sir Simon.

'Perhaps he's a robber himself,' suggested a lady.

'There is a curiously wild, wicked look about him, certainly, now that I examine him closely,' said the old mother.

Hubert blushed with shame; and, instead of continuing his story, and relating that robbers were concealed in the house, he doggedly held his tongue, and half resolved to let them find out their danger for themselves.

'Well, untie him,' said Sir Simon. 'Come, since it is Christmas Eve, we'll treat him well. Here, my lad; sit down in that empty seat at the bottom of the table, and make as good a meal as you can. When you have had your fill we will listen to more particulars of your story.'

The feast then proceeded; and Hubert, now at liberty, was not at all sorry to join in. The more they ate and drank the merrier did the company become; the wine flowed freely, the logs flared up the chimney, the ladies laughed at the gentlemen's stories; in short, all went as noisily and as happily as a Christmas gathering in old times possibly could do.

Hubert, in spite of his hurt feelings at their doubts of his honesty, could not help being warmed both in mind and in body by the good cheer, the scene, and the example of hilarity set by his neighbours. At last he laughed as heartily at their stories and repartees as the old **Baronet**, Sir Simon, himself. When the meal was almost over one of the sons, who had drunk a little too much wine, after the manner of men in that century, said to Hubert, 'Well my boy, how are you? Can you take a pinch of **snuff**?' He held out one of the snuff-boxes which were then becoming common among young and old throughout the country.

'Thank you,' said Hubert, accepting a pinch.

'Tell the ladies who you are, what you are made of, and what you can do,' the young man continued, slapping Hubert upon the shoulder.

'Certainly,' said our hero, drawing himself up, and thinking it best to put a bold face on the matter. 'I am a travelling magician.'

'Indeed!'

'What shall we hear next?'

'Can you call up spirits from the vasty deep, young wizard?'

'I can conjure up a **tempest** in a cupboard,' Hubert replied.

Baronet: hereditary knight/nobleman

snuff: powdered tobacco inhaled through the nose

tempest: storm

Hubert works his magic upon the cupboard

'Ha-ha!' said the old Baronet, pleasantly rubbing his hands. 'We must see this performance. Girls, don't go away: here's something to be seen.'

'Not dangerous, I hope?' said the old lady.

Hubert rose from the table. 'Hand me your snuff-box, please,' he said to the young man who had made free with him. 'And now,' he continued, 'without the least noise, follow me. If any of you speak it will break the spell.'

They promised obedience. He entered the corridor, and, taking off his shoes, went on tiptoe to the cupboard door, the guests advancing in a silent group at a little distance behind him. Hubert next placed a stool in front of the door, and, by standing upon it, was tall enough to reach the top. He then, just as noiselessly, poured all the snuff from the box along the upper edge of the door, and, with a few short puffs of breath, blew the snuff through the chink into the interior of the cupboard. He held up his finger to the assembly, that they might be silent.

'Dear me, what's that?' said the old lady, after a minute or two had elapsed.

A suppressed sneeze had come from inside the cupboard.

Hubert held up his finger again.

'How very **singular**,' whispered Sir Simon. 'This is most interesting.'

Hubert took advantage of the moment to gently slide the bolt of the cupboard into its place. 'More snuff,' he said, calmly.

'More snuff,' said Sir Simon. Two or three gentlemen passed their boxes, and the contents were

---

singular: unusual

blown in at the top of the cupboard. Another sneeze, not quite so well suppressed as the first, was heard: then another, which seemed to say that it would not be suppressed under any circumstances whatever. At length there arose a perfect storm of sneezes.

'Excellent, excellent for one so young!' said Sir Simon. 'I am much interested in this trick of throwing the voice – called, I believe, ventriloquism.'

'More snuff,' said Hubert.

'More snuff,' said Sir Simon. Sir Simon's man brought a large jar of the best scented Scotch.

Hubert once more charged the upper chink of the cupboard, and blew the snuff into the interior, as before. Again he charged, and again, emptying the whole contents of the jar. The tumult of sneezes became really extraordinary to listen to – there was **no cessation**. It was like wind, rain, and sea battling in a hurricane.

'I believe there are men inside, and that it is no trick at all!' exclaimed Sir Simon, the truth flashing on him.

'There are,' said Hubert. 'They are come to rob the house; and they are the same who stole my horse.'

The sneezes changed to **spasmodic groans**. One of the thieves, hearing Hubert's voice, cried, 'Oh! mercy! mercy! let us out of this!'

'Where's my horse?' cried Hubert.

'Tied to the tree in the hollow behind Short's Gibbet. Mercy! Mercy! let us out, or we shall die of suffocation!'

All the Christmas guests now perceived that this was no longer sport, but serious earnest. Guns and cudgels were procured; all the menservants were called in, and arranged in position outside the cupboard. At a signal Hubert withdrew the bolt, and stood on the defensive. But the three robbers, far from attacking them, were found crouching in the corner, gasping for breath.

They made no resistance; and, being pinioned, were placed in an outhouse till the morning.

Hubert now gave the remainder of his story to the assembled company, and was profusely thanked for the services he had rendered. Sir Simon pressed him to stay over the night, and accept the use of the best bedroom the house afforded, which had been occupied by Queen Elizabeth and King Charles successively when on their visits to this part of the country. But Hubert declined, being anxious to find his horse Jerry, and to test the truth of the robbers' statements concerning him.

Several of the guests accompanied Hubert to the spot behind the gibbet, alluded to by the thieves as where Jerry was hidden. When they reached the knoll and looked over, behold! there the horse stood, uninjured, and quite unconcerned. At the sight of Hubert he neighed joyfully: and nothing could exceed Hubert's gladness at finding him. He mounted, wished his friends 'Good night!' and cantered off in the direction they pointed out, reaching home safely about four o'clock in the morning.

---

no cessation: no stopping
spasmodic groans: occasional moans

The Blue Carbuncle

Sir Arthur Conan Doyle, 1859–1930

Sir Arthur Conan Doyle created the famous characters of Sherlock Holmes and Dr Watson. You may have seen film or television dramatizations of their exploits. It is easy to conjure up a picture of them discussing a crime in the comfort of 221B Baker Street. Even Dr Watson was often amazed by Holmes' powers of deduction and his solving of the apparently insoluble. Holmes did not have all the scientific equipment available to detectives nowadays, so he relied on close observation and made remarkably accurate deductions, often declaring that the solution was 'Elementary, my dear Watson!'

When Sherlock Holmes is brought an abandoned Christmas goose and a battered hat, it doesn't look like one of his most mysterious cases. But Holmes soon discovers that there is more to this particular goose than meets the eye . . .

I had called upon my friend Sherlock Holmes upon the second morning after Christmas, with the intention of wishing him the compliments of the season. He was lounging upon the sofa in a purple dressing-gown, a pipe-rack within his reach upon the right, and a pile of crumpled morning papers, evidently newly studied, near at hand. Beside the couch was a wooden chair, and on the angle of the back hung a very seedy and disreputable hard felt hat, much the worse for wear, and cracked in several places. A lens and **forceps** lying upon the seat of the chair suggested that the hat had been suspended in this manner for the purpose of examination.

'You are engaged,' said I; 'perhaps I interrupt you.'

'Not at all. I am glad to have a friend with whom I can discuss my results. The matter is a perfectly trivial one' (he jerked his thumb in the direction of the old hat), 'but there are points in connection with it which are not entirely devoid of interest, and even of instruction.'

I seated myself in his arm-chair, and warmed my hands before his crackling fire, for a sharp frost had set in, and the windows were thick with the ice crystals. 'I suppose,' I remarked, 'that, homely as it looks, this thing has some deadly story linked on to it – that it is the clue which will guide you in the solution of some mystery, and the punishment of some crime.'

'No, no. No crime,' said Sherlock Holmes, laughing. 'Only one of those **whimsical** little incidents which will happen when you have four million human beings all jostling each other within the space of a few square miles. Amid the action and reaction of so dense a swarm of humanity, every possible combination of events may be expected to take place, and many a little problem will be presented which may be striking and bizarre without being criminal. We have already had experience of such.'

'So much so,' I remarked, 'that, of the last six cases which I have added to my notes, three have been entirely free of any legal crime.'

'Precisely. You allude to my attempt to recover the Irene Adler papers, to the singular case of Miss Mary Sutherland, and to the adventure of the man with the

---

forceps: medical instrument for holding small objects
whimsical: humorous

Sherlock Holmes was lounging upon the sofa

twisted lip. Well, I have no doubt that this small matter will fall into the same innocent category. You know Peterson, the **commissionaire**?'

'Yes.'

'It is to him that this trophy belongs.'

'It is his hat.'

'No, no; he found it. Its owner is unknown. I beg that you will look upon it, not as a battered **billycock**, but as an intellectual problem. And, first as to how it came here. It arrived upon Christmas morning, in company with a good fat goose, which is, I have no doubt, roasting at this moment in front of Peterson's fire. The facts are these. About four o'clock on Christmas morning, Peterson, who, as you know, is a very honest fellow, was returning from some small jollification, and was making his way homewards down Tottenham Court Road. In front of him he saw, in the gaslight, a tallish man, walking with a light stagger, and carrying a white goose slung over his shoulder. As he reached the corner of Goodge Street a row broke out between this stranger and a little knot of roughs. One of the latter knocked off the man's hat, on which he raised his stick to defend himself, and, swinging it over his head, smashed the shop window behind him. Peterson had rushed forward to protect the stranger from his assailants, but the man, shocked at having broken the window and seeing an official-looking person in uniform rushing towards him, dropped his goose, took to his heels, and vanished amid the **labyrinth** of small streets which lie at the back of Tottenham Court Road.

---

commissionaire: doorman, caretaker
billycock: round, shallow felt hat
labyrinth: maze

The roughs had also fled at the appearance of Peterson, so that he was left in possession of the field of battle, and also of the spoils of victory in the shape of this battered hat and a most **unimpeachable** Christmas goose.'

'Which surely he restored to their owner?'

'My dear fellow, there lies the problem. It is true that "For Mrs Henry Baker" was printed upon a small card which was tied to the bird's left leg, and it is also true that the initials "H.B." are legible upon the lining of this hat; but, as there are some thousands of Bakers, and some hundreds of Henry Bakers in this city of ours, it is not easy to restore lost property to any one of them.'

'What, then, did Peterson do?'

'He brought round both hat and goose to me on Christmas morning, knowing that even the smallest problems are of interest to me. The goose we retained until this morning, when there were signs that, in spite of the slight frost, it would be well that it should be eaten without unnecessary delay. Its finder has carried it off therefore to fulfil the ultimate destiny of a goose, while I continue to retain the hat of the unknown gentleman who lost his Christmas dinner.'

'Did he not advertise?'

'No.'

'Then, what clue could you have as to his identity?'

'Only as much as we can **deduce**.'

'From his hat?'

'Precisely.'

'But you are joking. What can you gather from this old battered felt?'

'Here is my lens. You know my methods. What can you gather yourself as to the individuality of the man who has worn this article?'

I took the tattered object in my hands, and turned it over rather ruefully. It was a very ordinary black hat of the usual round shape, hard and much the worse for wear. The lining had been of red silk, but was a good deal discoloured. There was no maker's name; but, as Holmes had remarked, the initials 'H.B.' were scrawled upon one side. It was pierced in the brim for a hat-securer, but the elastic was missing. For the rest, it was cracked, exceedingly dusty, and spotted in several places, although there seemed to have been some attempt to hide the discoloured patches by smearing them with ink.

'I can see nothing,' said I, handing it back to my friend.

'On the contrary, Watson, you can see everything. You fail, however, to reason from what you see. You are too timid in drawing your **inferences**.'

'Then, pray tell me what it is that you can infer from this hat?'

He picked it up, and gazed at it in the peculiar **introspective** fashion which was characteristic of him. 'It is perhaps less suggestive than it might have been,' he remarked, 'and yet there are a few inferences which are very distinct, and a few others which represent at least a strong balance of probability. That the man was highly **intellectual** is of course obvious upon the face of it, and also that he was fairly

---

unimpeachable: innocent
deduce: work out, reason
inferences: conclusions
introspective: thoughtful, private
intellectual: clever

well-to-do within the last three years, although he has now fallen upon evil days. He had **foresight**, but has less now than formerly, pointing to a moral **retrogression**, which, when taken with the decline of his fortunes, seems to indicate some evil influence, probably drink, at work upon him. This may account also for the obvious fact that his wife has ceased to love him.'

'My dear Holmes!'

'He has, however, retained some degree of self-respect,' he continued, disregarding my **remonstrance**. 'He is a man who leads a **sedentary** life, goes out little, is out of training entirely, is middle-aged, has grizzled hair which he has had cut within the last few days, and which he anoints with lime-cream. These are the more patent facts which are to be deduced from his hat. Also, by the way, that it is extremely improbable that he has gas laid on in his house.'

'You are certainly joking, Holmes.'

'Not in the least. Is it possible that even now when I give you these results you are unable to see how they are attained?'

'I have no doubt that I am very stupid; but I must confess that I am unable to follow you. For example, how did you deduce that this man was intellectual?'

For answer Holmes clapped the hat upon his head. It came right over the forehead and settled upon the bridge of his nose. 'It is a question of **cubic capacity**,' said he: 'a man with so large a brain must have something in it.'

'The decline of his fortunes, then?'

'This hat is three years old. These flat brims curled at the edge came in then. It is a hat of the very best quality. Look at the band of ribbed silk, and the excellent lining. If this man could afford to buy so expensive a hat three years ago, and has had no hat since, then he has assuredly gone down in the world.'

'Well, that is clear enough, certainly. But how about the foresight, and the moral retrogression?'

Sherlock Holmes laughed. 'Here is the foresight,' said he, putting his finger upon the little disc and loop of the hat-securer. 'They are never sold upon hats. If this man ordered one, it is a sign of a certain amount of foresight, since he went out of his way to take this precaution against the wind. But since we see that he has broken the elastic, and has not troubled to replace it, it is obvious that he has less foresight now than formerly, which is a distinct proof of a weakening nature. On the other hand, he has endeavoured to conceal some of these stains upon the felt by daubing them with ink, which is a sign that he has not entirely lost his self-respect.'

'Your reasoning is certainly plausible.'

'The further points, that he is middle-aged, that his hair is grizzled, that it has been recently cut, and that he uses lime-cream, are all to be gathered from a close examination of the lower part of the lining. The lens discloses a large number of hair-ends, clean cut by the scissors of the barber. They all appear to be adhesive, and there is a distinct odour of lime-cream. This dust, you will observe, is not the gritty, grey dust of the street, but the fluffy brown dust of the house, showing

---

foresight: care for the future

retrogression: decline

remonstrance: protest

sedentary: inactive

cubic capacity: size, volume

that it has been hung up indoors most of the time; while the marks of moisture upon the inside are proof positive that the wearer perspired very freely, and could, therefore, hardly be in the best of training.'

'But his wife – you said that she had ceased to love him.'

'This hat has not been brushed for weeks. When I see you, my dear Watson, with a week's accumulation of dust upon your hat, and when your wife allows you to go out in such a state, I shall fear that you also have been unfortunate enough to lose your wife's affection.'

'But he might be a bachelor.'

'Nay, he was bringing home the goose as a peace-offering to his wife. Remember the card upon the bird's leg.'

'You have an answer to everything. But how on earth do you deduce that the gas is not laid on in the house?'

'One **tallow** stain, or even two, might come by chance; but, when I see no less than five, I think that there can be little doubt that the individual must be brought into frequent contact with burning tallow – walks upstairs at night probably with his hat in one hand and a guttering candle in the other. Anyhow, he never got tallow stains from a gas jet. Are you satisfied?'

'Well, it is very ingenious,' said I, laughing; 'but since, as you said just now, there has been no crime committed, and no harm done save the loss of a goose, all this seems to be rather a waste of energy.'

Sherlock Holmes had opened his mouth to reply, when the door flew open, and Peterson the commissionaire rushed into the compartment with flushed cheeks and the face of a man who is dazed with astonishment.

'The goose, Mr Holmes! The goose, sir!' he gasped.

'Eh! What of it, then? Has it returned to life, and flapped off through the kitchen window?' Holmes twisted himself round upon the sofa to get a fairer view of the man's excited face.

'See here, sir! See what my wife found in its crop!' He held out his hand, and displayed upon the centre of the palm a brilliantly scintillating blue stone, rather smaller than a bean in size, but of such purity and radiance that it twinkled like an electric point in the dark hollow of his hand.

Sherlock Holmes sat up with a whistle. 'By Jove, Peterson,' said he, 'this is treasure-trove indeed! I suppose you know what you have got?'

'A diamond, sir! A precious stone! It cuts into glass as though it were putty.'

'It's more than a precious stone. It's *the* precious stone.'

'Not the Countess of Morcar's blue carbuncle?' I ejaculated.

'Precisely so. I ought to know its size and shape, seeing that I have read the advertisement about it in *The Times* every day lately. It is absolutely unique, and its value can only be **conjectured**, but the reward offered of a thousand pounds is certainly not within a twentieth part of the market price.'

'A thousand pounds! Great Lord of mercy!' The commissionaire plumped down into a chair, and stared from one to the other of us.

'That is the reward, and I have reason to know that there are sentimental considerations in the back-

---

tallow: candle wax
conjectured: guessed, estimated

ground which would induce the Countess to part with half of her fortune if she could but recover the gem.'

'It was lost, if I remember aright, at the Hotel Cosmopolitan,' I remarked.

'Precisely so, on the twenty-second of December, just five days ago. John Horner, a plumber, was accused of having abstracted it from the lady's jewel-case. The evidence against him was so strong that the case has been referred to the Assizes. I have some account of the matter here, I believe.' He rummaged amid his newspapers, glancing over the dates, until at last he smoothed one out, doubled it over, and read the following paragraph:

'Hotel Cosmopolitan Jewel Robbery. John Horner, 26, plumber, was brought up upon the charge of having upon the 22nd inst., abstracted from the jewel-case of the Countess of Morcar the valuable gem known as the blue carbuncle. James Ryder, upper-attendant at the hotel, gave his evidence to the effect that he had shown Horner up to the dressing-room of the Countess of Morcar upon the day of the robbery, in order that he might solder the second bar of the grate, which was loose. He had remained with Horner some little time but had finally been called away. On returning he found that Horner had disappeared, that the bureau had been forced open, and that the small morocco casket in which, as it afterwards **transpired**, the Countess was accustomed to keep her jewel, was lying empty upon the dressing-table. Ryder instantly gave the alarm, and Horner was arrested the same evening; but the stone could not be found either upon his person or in his rooms. Catherine Cusack, maid to the Countess, deposed to having heard Ryder's cry of dismay on discovering the robbery, and to having rushed into the room, where she found matters were as described by the last witness. Inspector Bradstreet, B Division, gave evidence as to the arrest of Horner, who struggled frantically, and protested his innocence in the strongest terms. Evidence of a previous conviction for robbery having been given against the prisoner, the magistrate refused to deal **summarily** with the offence, but referred it to the Assizes. Horner, who had shown signs of intense emotion during the proceedings, fainted away at the conclusion, and was carried out of court.'

'Hum! So much for the police-court,' said Holmes thoughtfully, tossing aside his paper. 'The question for us now to solve is the sequence of events leading from a rifled jewel-case at one end to the crop of a goose in Tottenham Court Road at the other. You see, Watson, our little deductions have suddenly assumed a much more important and less innocent aspect. Here is the stone; the stone came from the goose, and the goose came from Mr Henry Baker, the gentleman with the bad hat and all the other characteristics with which I have bored you. So now we must set ourselves very seriously to finding this gentleman, and ascertaining what part he has played in this little mystery. To do this, we must try the simplest means first, and these lie undoubtedly in an advertisement in all the evening papers. If this fails, I shall have recourse to other methods.'

'What will you say?'

'Give me a pencil, and that slip of paper. Now, then: "Found at the corner of Goodge Street, a goose and a black felt hat. Mr Henry Baker can have the same by

---

transpired: turned out
summarily: without delay

applying at 6.30 this evening at 221B Baker Street."
That is clear and concise.'

'Very. But will he see it?'

'Well, he is sure to keep an eye on the papers, since,
to a poor man, the loss was a heavy one. He was clearly
so scared by his mischance in breaking the window,
and by the approach of Peterson, that he thought of
nothing but flight; but since then he must have
bitterly regretted the impulse which caused him to
drop his bird. Then, again, the introduction of his
name will cause him to see it, for every one who knows
him will direct his attention to it. Here you are,
Peterson, run down to the advertising agency, and
have this put in the evening papers.'

'In which, sir?'

'Oh, in the *Globe, Star, Pall Mall, St. James'
Gazette, Evening News, Standard, Echo,* and any
others that occur to you.'

'Very well, sir. And this stone?'

'Ah, yes, I shall keep the stone. Thank you. And, I
say, Peterson, just buy a goose on your way back, and
leave it here with me, for we must have one to give to
this gentleman in place of the one which your family is
now devouring.'

When the commissionaire had gone, Holmes took up
the stone and held it against the light. 'It's a bonny
thing,' said he. 'Just see how it glints and sparkles. Of
course it is a nucleus and focus of crime. Every good
stone is. They are the devil's pet baits. In the larger
and older jewels every facet may stand for a bloody
deed. This stone is not yet twenty years old. It was
found in the banks of the Amoy River in Southern
China, and is remarkable in having every
characteristic of the carbuncle, save that it is blue in
shade, instead of ruby red. In spite of its youth, it has

already a sinister history. There have been two murders, a **vitriol**-throwing, a suicide, and several robberies brought about for the sake of this forty-grain weight of crystallized charcoal. Who would think that so pretty a toy would be a purveyor to the gallows and the prison? I'll lock it up in my strong-box now, and drop a line to the Countess to say that we have it.'

'Do you think this man Horner is innocent?'

'I cannot tell.'

'Well, then, do you imagine that this other one, Henry Baker, had anything to do with the matter?'

'It is, I think, much more likely that Henry Baker is an absolutely innocent man, who had no idea that the bird which he was carrying was of considerably more value than if it were made of solid gold. That, however, I shall determine by a very simple test, if we have an answer to our advertisement.'

'And you can do nothing until then?'

'Nothing.'

'In that case I shall continue my professional round. But I shall come back in the evening at the hour you have mentioned, for I should like to see the solution of so tangled a business.'

'Very glad to see you. I dine at seven. There is a woodcock, I believe. By the way, in view of recent occurrences, perhaps I ought to ask Mrs Hudson to examine its crop.'

I had been delayed at a case, and it was a little after half-past six when I found myself in Baker Street once more. As I approached the house I saw a tall man in a Scotch bonnet, with a coat which was buttoned up to his chin, waiting outside in the bright semicircle which

---

vitriol: sulphuric acid

was thrown from the fanlight. Just as I arrived, the door was opened, and we were shown up together to Holmes' room.

'Mr Henry Baker, I believe,' said he, rising from his arm-chair, and greeting his visitor with the easy air of geniality which he could so readily assume. 'Pray take this chair by the fire, Mr Baker. It is a cold night, and I observe that your circulation is more adapted for summer than for winter. Ah, Watson, you have just come at the right time. Is that your hat, Mr Baker?'

'Yes, sir, that is undoubtedly my hat.'

He was a large man, with rounded shoulders, a massive head, and a broad, intelligent face, sloping down to a pointed beard of grizzled brown. A touch of red in nose and cheeks, with a slight tremor of his extended hand, recalled Holmes' surmise as to his habits. His rusty black frock-coat was buttoned right up in front, with the collar turned up, and his lank wrists protruded from his sleeves without a sign of cuff or shirt. He spoke in a low staccato fashion, choosing his words with care, and gave the impression generally of a man of learning and letters who had had ill-usage at the hands of fortune.

'We have retained these things for some days,' said Holmes, 'because we expected to see an advertisement from you giving your address. I am at a loss to know now why you did not advertise.'

Our visitor gave a rather shamefaced laugh. 'Shillings have not been so plentiful with me as they once were,' he remarked. 'I had no doubt that the gang of roughs who assaulted me had carried off both my hat and the bird. I did not care to spend more money in a hopeless attempt at recovering them.'

'Very naturally. By the way, about the bird – we were compelled to eat it.'

'To eat it!' Our visitor half rose from his chair in his excitement.

'Yes; it would have been no use to anyone had we not done so. But I presume that this other goose upon the sideboard, which is about the same weight and perfectly fresh, will answer your purpose equally well?'

'Oh, certainly, certainly!' answered Mr Baker, with a sigh of relief.

'Of course, we still have the feathers, legs, crop, and so on of your own bird, if you so wish –'

The man burst into a hearty laugh. 'They might be useful to me as relics of my adventure,' said he, 'but beyond that I can hardly see what use the *disjecta membra* of my late acquaintance are going to be to me. No, sir, I think that, with your permission, I will confine my attentions to the excellent bird which I perceive upon the sideboard.'

Sherlock Holmes glanced across at me with a slight shrug of his shoulders.

'There is your hat, then, and there your bird,' said he. 'By the way, would it bore you to tell me where you got the other one from? I am somewhat of a fowl fancier, and I have seldom seen a better-grown goose.'

'Certainly, sir,' said Baker, who had risen and tucked his newly gained property under his arm. 'There are a few of us who frequent the Alpha Inn near the Museum – we are to be found in the Museum itself during the day, you understand. This year our good host, Windigate by name, instituted a goose-club, by which, on consideration of some few pence every week, we were to receive a bird at Christmas. My pence were duly paid, and the rest is familiar to you. I am much

---

disjecta membra: scattered remains

indebted to you, sir, for a Scotch bonnet is fitted neither to my years nor my gravity.' With a comical pomposity of manner he bowed solemnly to both of us, and strode off upon his way.

'So much for Mr Henry Baker,' said Holmes, when he had closed the door behind him. 'It is quite certain that he knows nothing whatever about the matter. Are you hungry, Watson?'

'Not particularly.'

'Then I suggest that we turn our dinner into a supper, and follow up this clue while it is still hot.'

'By all means.'

It was a bitter night, so we drew on our **ulsters** and wrapped cravats about our throats. Outside, the stars were shining coldly in a cloudless sky, and the breath of the passers-by blew out into smoke like so many pistol shots. Our footfalls rang out crisply and loudly as we swung through the doctors' quarter, Wimpole Street, Harley Street, and so through Wigmore Street into Oxford Street. In a quarter of an hour we were in Bloomsbury at the Alpha Inn, which is a small public-house at the corner of one of the streets which run down into Holborn. Holmes pushed open the door of the private bar, and ordered two glasses of beer from the ruddy-faced, white-aproned landlord.

'Your beer should be excellent if it is as good as your geese,' he said.

'My geese!' The man seemed surprised.

'Yes. I was speaking only half an hour ago to Mr Henry Baker, who was a member of your goose-club.'

'Ah! yes, I see. But you see, sir, them's not *our* geese.'

'Indeed! Whose, then?'

'Well, I get the two dozen from a salesman in Covent Garden.'

'Indeed! I know some of them. Which was it?'

'Breckinridge is his name.'

'Ah! I don't know him. Well, here's your good health, landlord, and prosperity to your house. Good night.'

'Now for Mr Breckinridge', he continued, buttoning up his coat, as we came out into the frosty air. 'Remember, Watson, that though we have so homely a thing as a goose at one end of this chain, we have at the other a man who will certainly get seven years' penal servitude, unless we can establish his innocence. It is possible that our inquiry may but confirm his guilt; but, in any case, we have a line of investigation which has been missed by the police, and which a singular chance has placed in our hands. Let us follow it out to the bitter end. Faces to the south, then, and quick march!'

We passed across Holborn, down Endell Street, and so through a zigzag of slums to Covent Garden Market. One of the largest stalls bore the name of Breckinridge upon it, and the proprietor, a horsy-looking man, with a sharp face and trim side-whiskers, was helping a boy to put up the shutters.

'Good evening. It's a cold night,' said Holmes.

The salesman nodded, and shot a questioning glance at my companion.

'Sold out of geese, I see,' continued Holmes, pointing at the bare slabs of marble.

'Let you have five hundred tomorrow morning.'

'That's no good.'

'Well, there are some on the stall with the gas flare.'

'Ah, but I was recommended to you.'

'Who by?'

'The landlord of the "Alpha".'

---

ulster: long, loose overcoat

'Ah, yes; I sent him a couple of dozen.'

'Fine birds they were, too. Now where did you get them from?'

To my surprise the question provoked a burst of anger from the salesman.

'Now then, mister,' said he, with his head cocked and his arms akimbo, 'what are you driving at? Let's have it straight, now.'

'It is straight enough. I should like to know who sold you the geese which you supplied to the "Alpha".'

'Well, then, I shan't tell you. So now!'

'Oh, it is a matter of no importance; but I don't know why you should be so warm over such a trifle.'

'Warm! You'd be as warm, maybe, if you were as pestered as I am. When I pay good money for a good article there should be an end to the business; but it's "Where are the geese?" and "Who did you sell the geese to?" and "What will you take for the geese?" One would think they were the only geese in the world, to hear the fuss that is made over them.'

'Well, I have no connection with any other people who have been making inquiries,' said Holmes carelessly. 'If you won't tell us the bet is off, that is all. But I'm always ready to back my opinion on a matter of fowls, and I have a fiver on it that the bird I ate is country bred.'

'Well, then, you've lost your fiver, for it's town bred,' snapped the salesman.

'It's nothing of the kind.'

'I say it is.'

'I don't believe you.'

'D'you think you know more about fowls than I, who have handled them ever since I was a nipper? I tell you, all those birds that went to the "Alpha" were town bred.'

'You'll never persuade me to believe that.'

'Will you bet, then?'

'It's merely taking your money, for I know that I am right. But I'll have a sovereign on with you, just to teach you not to be obstinate.'

The salesman chuckled grimly. 'Bring me the books, Bill,' said he.

The small boy brought round a small thin volume and a great greasy-backed one, laying them out together beneath the hanging lamp.

'Now then, Mr Cocksure,' said the salesman, 'I thought that I was out of geese, but before I finish you'll find that there is still one left in my shop. You see this little book?'

'Well?'

'That's the list of the folk from whom I buy. D'you see? Well, then, here on this page are the country folk, and the numbers after their names are where their accounts are in the big ledger. Now, then! You see this other page in red ink? Well, that is a list of my town suppliers. Now, look at that third name. Just read it out to me.'

'"Mrs Oakshott, 117 Brixton Road – 249,"' read Holmes.

'Quite so. Now turn that up in the ledger.'

Holmes turned to the page indicated. 'Here you are, "Mrs Oakshott, 117 Brixton Road, egg and poultry supplier."'

'Now, then, what's the last entry?'

'"December 22. Twenty-four geese at 7s. 6d."'

'Quite so. There you are. And underneath?'

'"Sold to Mr Windigate of the 'Alpha' at 12s."'

'What have you to say now?'

Sherlock Holmes looked deeply **chagrined**. He drew a sovereign from his pocket and threw it down upon

---

chagrined: disappointed

the slab, turning away with the air of a man whose disgust is too deep for words. A few yards off he stopped under a lamp-post, and laughed in the hearty, noiseless fashion which was peculiar to him.

'When you see a man with whiskers of that cut and the "**Pink 'Un**" protruding out of his pocket, you can always draw him by a bet,' said he. 'I dare say that if I had put a hundred pounds down in front of him that man would not have given me such complete information as was drawn from him by the idea that he was doing me on a wager. Well, Watson, we are, I fancy, nearing the end of our quest, and the only point which remains to be determined is whether we should go on to this Mrs Oakshott tonight, or whether we should reserve it for tomorrow. It is clear from what that surly fellow said that there are others besides ourselves who are anxious about the matter, and I should –'

His remarks were suddenly cut short by a loud hubbub which broke out from the stall which we had just left. Turning round we saw a little rat-faced fellow standing in the centre of the circle of yellow light which was thrown by the swinging lamp, while Breckinridge the salesman, framed in the door of his stall, was shaking his fists fiercely at the cringing figure.

'I've had enough of you and your geese,' he shouted. 'I wish you were all at the devil together. If you come pestering me any more with your silly talk I'll set the dog at you. You bring Mrs Oakshott here and I'll answer her, but what have you to do with it? Did I buy the geese off you?'

'No; but one of them was mine all the same,' whined the little man.

'Well, then, ask Mrs Oakshott for it.'

'She told me to ask you.'

'Well, you can ask the King of Proosia, for all I care. I've had enough of it. Get out of this!' He rushed fiercely forward, and the inquirer flitted away into the darkness.

'Ha, this may save us a visit to Brixton Road,' whispered Holmes. 'Come with me, and we will see what is to be made of this fellow.' Striding through the scattered knots of people who lounged round the flaring stalls, my companion speedily overtook the little man and touched him upon the shoulder. He sprang round, and I could see in the gaslight that every **vestige** of colour had been driven from his face.

'Who are you, then? What do you want?' he asked in a quavering voice.

'You will excuse me,' said Holmes blandly, 'but I could not help overhearing the questions which you put to the salesman just now. I think that I could be of assistance to you.'

'You? Who are you? How could you know anything of the matter?'

'My name is Sherlock Holmes. It is my business to know what other people don't know.'

'But you can know nothing of this!'

'Excuse me, I know everything of it. You are endeavouring to trace some geese which were sold by Mrs Oakshott, of Brixton Road, to a salesman named Breckinridge, by him in turn to Mr Windigate, of the "Alpha," and by him to his club, of which Mr Henry Baker is a member.'

'Oh, sir, you are the very man whom I have longed to meet,' cried the little fellow, with outstretched

---

'Pink 'Un': racing newspaper

vestige: trace

hands and quivering fingers. 'I can hardly explain to you how interested I am in this matter.'

Sherlock Holmes hailed a four-wheeler which was passing. 'In that case we had better discuss it in a cosy room rather than in this wind-swept market-place,' said he. 'But pray tell me, before we go further, who it is that I have the pleasure of assisting.'

The man hesitated for an instant. 'My name is John Robinson,' he answered, with a sidelong glance.

'No, no; the real name,' said Holmes sweetly. 'It is always awkward doing business with an *alias*.'

A flush sprang to the white cheeks of the stranger. 'Well, then,' said he, 'my real name is James Ryder.'

'Precisely so. Head attendant at the Hotel Cosmopolitan. Pray step into the cab, and I shall soon be able to tell you everything which you would wish to know.'

The little man stood glancing from one to the other of us with half-frightened, half-hopeful eyes, as one who is not sure whether he is on the verge of a windfall or of a catastrophe. Then he stepped into the cab, and in half an hour we were back in the sitting-room at Baker Street. Nothing had been said during our drive, but the high, thin breathings of our new companion, and the claspings and unclaspings of his hands, spoke of the nervous tension within him.

'Here we are!' said Holmes cheerily, as we filed into the room. 'The fire looks very seasonable in this weather. You look cold, Mr Ryder. Pray take the basket chair. I will just put on my slippers before we settle this little matter of yours. Now, then! You want to know what became of those geese?'

'Yes, sir.'

'Or rather, I fancy, of that goose. It was one bird, I imagine, in which you were interested – white, with a black bar across the tail.'

Ryder quivered with emotion. 'Oh, sir,' he cried, 'can you tell me where it went to?'

'It came here.'

'Here?'

'Yes, and a most remarkable bird it proved. I don't wonder that you should take an interest in it. It laid an egg after it was dead – the bonniest, brightest little blue egg that ever was seen. I have it here in my museum.'

Our visitor staggered to his feet, and clutched the mantelpiece with his right hand. Holmes unlocked his strong-box, and held up the blue carbuncle, which shone out like a star, with a cold, brilliant, many-pointed radiance. Ryder stood glaring with a drawn face, uncertain whether to claim or to disown it.

'The game's up, Ryder,' said Holmes quietly. 'Hold up, man, or you'll be into the fire. Give him an arm back into his chair, Watson. He's not got blood enough to go in for **felony** with **impunity**. Give him a dash of brandy. So! Now he looks a little more human. What a shrimp it is, to be sure!'

For a moment he had staggered and nearly fallen, but the brandy brought a tinge of colour into his cheeks, and he sat staring with frightened eyes at his accuser.

'I have almost every link in my hands, and all the proofs which I could possibly need, so there is little which you need tell me. Still, that little may as well be cleared up to make the case complete. You had heard, Ryder, of this blue stone of the Countess of Morcar's?'

'It was Catherine Cusack who told me of it,' said he, in a crackling voice.

---

felony: crime
impunity: no punishment

'I see. Her ladyship's waiting-maid. Well, the temptation of sudden wealth so easily acquired was too much for you, as it has been for better men before you; but you were not very **scrupulous** in the means you used. It seems to me, Ryder, that there is the making of a very pretty villain in you. You knew that this man Horner, the plumber, had been concerned in some such matter before, and that suspicion would rest the more readily upon him. What did you do, then? You made some small job in my lady's room – you and your confederate Cusack – and you managed that he should be the man sent for. Then, when he had left, you rifled the jewel-case, raised the alarm, and had this unfortunate man arrested. You then –'

Ryder threw himself down suddenly upon the rug, and clutched at my companion's knees. 'For God's sake, have mercy!' he shrieked. 'Think of my father! Of my mother! It would break their hearts. I never went wrong before! I never will again. I swear it. I'll swear it on a Bible. Oh, don't bring it into court! For Christ's sake, don't!'

'Get back into your chair!' said Holmes sternly. 'It is very well to cringe and crawl now, but you thought little enough of this poor Horner in the dock for a crime of which he knew nothing.'

'I will fly, Mr Holmes. I will leave the country, sir. Then the charge against him will break down.'

'Hum! We will talk about that. And now let us hear a true account of the next act. How came the stone into the goose, and how came the goose into the open market? Tell us the truth, for there lies your only hope of safety.'

Ryder passed his tongue over his parched lips. 'I will tell you it just as it happened, sir,' said he. 'When Horner had been arrested, it seemed to me that it would be best for me to get away with the stone at once, for I did not know at what moment the police might not take it into their heads to search me and my room. There was no place about the hotel where it would be safe. I went out, as if on some commission, and I made for my sister's house. She had married a man named Oakshott, and lived in Brixton Road, where she fattened fowls for the market. All the way there every man I met seemed to me to be a policeman or a detective, and for all that it was a cold night, the sweat was pouring down my face before I came to the Brixton Road. My sister asked me what was the matter, and why I was so pale; but I told her that I had been upset by the jewel robbery at the hotel. Then I went into the back-yard, and smoked a pipe, and wondered what it would be best to do.

'I had a friend once called Maudsley, who went to the bad, and has just been serving his time in Pentonville. One day he had met me, and fell into talk about the ways of thieves and how they could get rid of what they stole. I knew that he would be true to me, for I knew one or two things about him, so I made up my mind to go right on to Kilburn, where he lived, and take him into my confidence. He would show me how to turn the stone into money. But how to get to him in safety? I thought of the agonies I had gone through in coming from the hotel. I might at any moment be seized and searched, and there would be the stone in my waistcoat pocket. I was leaning against the wall at the time, and looking at the geese which were waddling about round my feet, and suddenly an idea came into my head which showed me how I could beat the best detective that ever lived.

---

scrupulous: fair

I thrust the stone down its throat as far as my finger could reach

'My sister had told me some weeks before that I might have the pick of her geese for a Christmas present, and I knew that she was always as good as her word. I would take my goose now, and in it I would carry my stone to Kilburn. There was a little shed in the yard, and behind this I drove one of the birds, a fine big one, white, with a barred tail. I caught it and, prising its bill open, I thrust the stone down its throat as far as my finger could reach. The bird gave a gulp, and I felt the stone pass along its gullet and down into its crop. But the creature flapped and struggled, and out came my sister to know what was the matter. As I turned to speak to her the brute broke loose, and fluttered off among the others.

'"Whatever were you doing with that bird, Jem?" says she.

'"Well," said I, "you said you'd give me one for Christmas, and I was feeling which was the fattest."

'"Oh," says she, "we've set yours aside for you. Jem's bird, we call it. It's the big, white one over yonder. There's twenty-six of them, which makes one for you, and one for us, and two dozen for the market."

'"Thank you, Maggie," says I; "but if it is all the same to you I'd rather have that one I was handling just now."

'"The other is a good three pound heavier," she said, "and we fattened it expressly for you."

'"Never mind. I'll have the other, and I'll take it now," said I.

'"Oh, just as you like," said she, a little huffed. "Which is it you want, then?"

'"That white one, with the barred tail, right in the middle of the flock."

'"Oh, very well. Kill it and take it with you."'

'Well, I did what she said, Mr Holmes, and I carried the bird all the way to Kilburn. I told my pal what I had done, for he was a man that it was easy to tell a thing like that to. He laughed until he choked, and we got a knife and opened the goose. My heart turned to water, for there was no sign of the stone, and I knew that some terrible mistake had occurred. I left the bird, rushed back to my sister's, and hurried into the back-yard. There was not a bird to be seen there.

'"Where are they all, Maggie?" I cried.

'"Gone to the dealer's."

'"Which dealer's?"

'"Breckinridge, of Covent Garden."

'"But was there another with a barred tail?" I asked, "the same as the one I chose?"

'"Yes, Jem, there were two barred-tailed ones, and I could never tell them apart."

'Well, then, of course, I saw it all, and I ran off as hard as my feet would carry me to this man Breckinridge; but he had sold the lot at once, and not one word would he tell me as to where they had gone. You heard him yourselves to-night. Well, he has always answered me like that. My sister thinks that I am going mad. Sometimes I think that I am myself. And now – and now I am myself a branded thief, without ever having touched the wealth for which I sold my character. God help me! God help me!' He burst into convulsive sobbing, with his face buried in his hands.

There was a long silence, broken only by his heavy breathing, and by the measured tapping of Sherlock Holmes' finger-tips upon the edge of the table. Then my friend rose, and threw open the door.

'Get out!' said he.

'What, sir! Oh, Heaven bless you!'

'No more words. Get out!'

And no more words were needed. There was a rush, a clatter upon the stairs, the bang of a door, and the crisp rattle of running footfalls from the street.

'After all, Watson,' said Holmes, reaching up his hand for his clay pipe, 'I am not retained by the police to **supply their deficiencies**. If Horner were in danger it would be another thing, but this fellow will not appear against him, and the case must collapse. I suppose that I am **commuting a felony**, but it is just possible that I am saving a soul. This fellow will not go wrong again. He is too terribly frightened. Send him to gaol now, and you make him a gaolbird for life. Besides, it is the season of forgiveness. Chance has put in our way a most singular and whimsical problem, and its solution is its own reward. If you will have the goodness to touch the bell, Doctor, we will begin another investigation, in which also a bird will be the chief feature.'

---

supply their deficiencies: make up for their shortcomings
commuting a felony: exchanging one crime for another

The Monkey's Paw

W W Jacobs, 1863–1943

W W Jacobs was a Londoner who lived near the river and so he often included sailors and travellers in his stories. One such is Sergeant-Major Morris who, in the following story, brings back from his travels a souvenir which has unforeseen consequences.

In this dramatic mystery story, full of atmosphere and fore-boding, a family called White decide to keep the souvenir – a monkey's paw which will grant their wishes. When Mr White wishes for two hundred pounds the monkey's paw twists in his hand like a snake, and there is no turning back . . .

Without, the night was cold and wet, but in the small parlour of Laburnum Villa the blinds were drawn and the fire burned brightly. Father and son were at chess.

'Hark at the wind,' said Mr White.

'I'm listening,' said the son, grimly surveying the board as he stretched out his hand. 'Check.'

'I should hardly think that he'd come tonight,' said his father, with his hand **poised** over the board.

'Mate,' replied the son.

'That's the worst of living so far out,' bawled Mr White, with sudden and unlooked-for violence; 'of all the beastly, slushy, out-of-the-way places to live in, this is the worst. Path's a bog, and road's a torrent. I don't know what people are thinking about. I suppose because only two houses in the road are let, they think it doesn't matter.'

'Never mind, dear,' said his wife, soothingly; 'perhaps you will win the next one.'

Mr White looked up sharply, just in time to **intercept** a knowing glance between mother and son. The words died away on his lips, and he hid a guilty grin in his thin grey beard.

'There he is,' said Herbert White, as the gate banged to loudly and heavy footsteps came towards the door.

The old man rose with **hospitable haste**, and opening the door, was heard **condoling** with the new arrival. The new arrival also condoled with himself, so that Mrs White said, 'Tut, Tut!' and coughed gently as her husband entered the room, followed by a tall, burly man, beady of eye and **rubicund of visage**.

'Sergeant-Major Morris,' he said, introducing him.

The sergeant-major shook hands, and taking the proffered seat by the fire, watched contentedly while his host got out whisky and tumblers and stood a small copper kettle on the fire.

At the third glass his eyes got brighter, and he began to talk, the little family circle regarding with eager interest this visitor from distant parts, as he squared his broad shoulders in the chair and spoke of wild scenes and **doughty** deeds; of wars and plagues and strange peoples.

---

without: outside
poised: hovering
intercept: notice, catch
hospitable haste: friendly speed
condoling: sympathizing
rubicund of visage: red-faced
doughty: brave

Mrs White drew back with a grimace

'Twenty-one years of it,' said Mr White, nodding at his wife and son. 'When he went away he was a slip of a youth in the warehouse. Now look at him.'

'He don't look to have taken much harm,' said Mrs White politely.

'I'd like to go to India myself,' said the old man, 'just to look around a bit, you know.'

'Better where you are,' said the sergeant-major, shaking his head. He put down the empty glass, and, sighing softly, shook his head again.

'I should like to see those old temples and **fakirs** and jugglers,' said the old man. 'What was that you started telling me the other day about a monkey's paw or something, Morris?'

'Nothing,' said the soldier hastily. 'Leastways nothing worth hearing.'

'Monkey's paw?' said Mrs White curiously.

'Well, it's just a bit of what you might call magic, perhaps,' said the sergeant-major, offhandedly.

His three listeners leaned forward eagerly. The visitor absent-mindedly put his empty glass to his lips and then set it down again. His host filled it for him.

'To look at,' said the sergeant-major, fumbling in his pocket, 'it's just an ordinary little paw, dried to a **mummy**.'

He took something out of his pocket and proffered it. Mrs White drew back with a **grimace**, but her son, taking it, examined it curiously.

'And what is there special about it?' inquired Mr White as he took it from his son, and having examined it, placed it upon the table.

---

fakirs: holy men
mummy: preserved, shrivelled form
grimace: disgusted expression

'It had a spell put on it by an old fakir,' said the sergeant-major, 'a very holy man. He wanted to show that fate ruled people's lives, and that those who interfered with it did so to their sorrow. He put a spell on it so that three separate men could each have three wishes from it.'

His manner was so impressive that his hearers were conscious that their light laughter **jarred** somewhat.

'Well, why don't you have three, sir?' said Herbert White, cleverly.

The soldier regarded him in the way that middle age is wont to regard presumptuous youth.

'I have,' he said quietly, and his blotchy face whitened.

'And did you really have the three wishes granted?' asked Mrs White.

'I did,' said the sergeant-major, and his glass tapped against his strong teeth.

'And has anybody else wished?' persisted the old lady.

'The first man had his three wishes. Yes,' was the reply. 'I don't know what the first two were, but the third was for death. That's how I got the paw.'

His tones were so grave that a hush fell upon the group.

'If you've had your three wishes, it's no good to you now, then, Morris,' said the old man at last. 'What do you keep it for?'

The soldier shook his head. 'Fancy, I suppose,' he said slowly. 'I did have some idea of selling it, but I don't think I will. It has caused enough mischief already. Besides, people won't buy. They think it's a fairy tale, some of them; and those who do think anything of it want to try it first and pay me afterwards.'

'If you could have another three wishes,' said the old man, eyeing him keenly, 'would you have them?'

'I don't know,' said the other. 'I don't know.'

He took the paw, and dangling it between his forefinger and thumb, suddenly threw it upon the fire. White, with a slight cry, stooped down and snatched it off.

'Better let it burn,' said the soldier solemnly.

'If you don't want it, Morris,' said the other, 'give it to me.'

'I won't,' said his friend doggedly. 'I threw it on the fire. If you keep it, don't blame me for what happens. Pitch it on the fire again, like a sensible man.'

The other shook his head and examined his new possession closely. 'How do you do it?' he inquired.

'Hold it up in your right hand and wish aloud,' said the sergeant-major, 'but I warn you of the consequences.'

'Sounds like *Arabian Nights*,' said Mrs White, as she rose and began to set the supper. 'Don't you think you might wish for four pairs of hands for me?'

Her husband drew the **talisman** from his pocket, and then all three burst into laughter as the sergeant-major, with a look of alarm on his face, caught him by the arm.

'If you must wish,' he said gruffly, 'wish for something sensible.'

Mr White dropped it back in his pocket, and placing chairs, motioned his friend to the table. In the business of supper the talisman was partly forgotten, and afterwards the three sat listening in an enthralled

---

jarred: was out of place
talisman: charm

fashion to a second instalment of the soldier's adventures in India.

'If the tale about the monkey's paw is not more truthful than those he has been telling us,' said Herbert, as the door closed behind their guest, just in time to catch the last train, 'we shan't get much out of it.'

'Did you give him anything for it, father?' inquired Mrs White, regarding her husband closely.

'A trifle,' said he, colouring slightly. 'He didn't want it, but I made him take it. And he pressed me again to throw it away.'

'Likely,' said Herbert, with pretended horror. 'Why, we're going to be rich, and famous and happy. Wish to be an Emperor, father, to begin with; then you can't be henpecked.'

He darted round the table, pursued by the maligned Mrs White.

Mr White took the paw from his pocket and eyed it dubiously.

'I don't know what to wish for, and that's a fact,' he said, slowly.

'It seems to me I've got all I want.'

'If you only cleared the house, you'd be quite happy, wouldn't you?' said Herbert, with his hand on his shoulder. 'Well, wish for two hundred pounds then; that'll just do it.'

His father, smiling shamefacedly at his own **credulity**, held up the talisman, as his son, with a solemn face, somewhat marred by a wink at his mother, sat down at the piano and struck a few impressive chords.

'I wish for two hundred pounds,' said the old man distinctly.

A fine crash from the piano greeted the words, interrupted by a shuddering cry from the old man. His wife and son ran towards him.

'It moved,' he cried, with a glance of disgust at the object as it lay on the floor.

'As I wished, it twisted in my hand like a snake.'

'Well, I don't see the money,' said his son, as he picked it up and placed it on the table, 'and I bet I never shall.'

'It must have been your fancy, father,' said his wife, regarding him anxiously.

He shook his head. 'Never mind, though; there's no harm done, but it gave me a shock all the same.'

They sat down by the fire again while the two men finished their pipes. Outside, the wind was higher than ever, and the old man started nervously at the sound of a door banging upstairs. A silence unusual and depressing settled upon all three, which lasted until the old couple arose to retire for the night.

'I expect you'll find the cash tied up in a big bag in the middle of your bed,' said Herbert, as he bade them good night, 'and something horrible squatting up on top of your wardrobe watching you as you pocket your ill-gotten gains.'

He sat alone in the darkness, gazing at the dying fire, and seeing faces in it. The last face was so horrible that he gazed at it in amazement. It got so vivid that, with a little uneasy laugh, he felt on the table for a glass containing a little water to throw over it. His hand grasped the monkey's paw, and with a little shiver he wiped his hand on his coat and went up to bed.

In the brightness of the wintry sun next morning as it streamed over the breakfast table, he laughed at his fears. There was an air of **prosaic wholesomeness**

---

credulity: willingness to believe
prosaic wholesomeness: natural atmosphere

about the room which it had lacked on the previous night, and the dirty, shrivelled little paw was pitched on the sideboard with a carelessness which **betokened** no great belief in its virtues.

'I suppose all old soldiers are the same,' said Mrs White. 'The idea of our listening to such nonsense! How could wishes be granted in these days? And if they could, how could two hundred pounds hurt you, father?'

'Might drop on his head from the sky,' said the frivolous Herbert.

'Morris said the things happened so naturally,' said his father, 'that you might if you so wished attribute it to coincidence.'

'Well, don't break into the money before I come back,' said Herbert as he rose from the table. 'I'm afraid it'll turn you into a mean, **avaricious** man, and we shall have to disown you.'

His mother laughed, and following him to the door, watched him down the road; and returning to the breakfast table, was very merry at the expense of her husband's credulity. All of which did not prevent her from scurrying to the door at the postman's knock, nor prevent her from referring somewhat shortly to retired sergeant-majors of bibulous habits when she found that the post brought a tailor's bill.

'Herbert will have some more of his funny remarks, I expect, when he comes home,' she said, as they sat at dinner.

'I dare say,' said Mr White, pouring himself out some beer; 'but for all that, the thing moved in my hand; that I'll swear to.'

'You thought it did,' said the old lady soothingly.

'I say it did,' replied the other. 'There was no thought about it; I had just – What's the matter?'

His wife made no reply. She was watching the mysterious movements of a man outside, who, peering in an undecided fashion at the house, appeared to be trying to make up his mind to enter. In mental connection with the two hundred pounds, she noticed that the stranger was well dressed, and wore a silk hat of glossy newness. Three times he paused at the gate, and then walked on again. The fourth time he stood with his hand upon it, and then with sudden resolution flung it open and walked up the path. Mrs White at the same moment placed her hands behind her, and hurriedly unfastening the strings of her apron, put that useful article of apparel beneath the cushion of her chair.

She brought the stranger, who seemed ill at ease, into the room. He gazed at her furtively, and listened in a preoccupied fashion as the old lady apologized for the appearance of the room, and her husband's coat, a garment which he usually reserved for the garden. She then waited as patiently as her sex would permit, for him to broach his business, but he was at first strangely silent.

'I – was asked to call,' he said at last, and stooped and picked a piece of cotton from his trousers. 'I come from "Maw and Meggins".'

The old lady started. 'Is anything the matter?' she asked breathlessly. 'Has anything happened to Herbert? What is it?'

Her husband interposed. 'There, there, mother,' he said hastily. 'Sit down and don't jump to conclusions. You've not brought bad news, I'm sure, sir'; and he eyed the other wistfully.

---

betokened: indicated, showed
avaricious: greedy

'I'm sorry –' began the visitor.

'Is he hurt?' demanded the mother wildly.

The visitor bowed in assent. 'Badly hurt,' he said quietly, 'but he is not in any pain.'

'Oh, thank God!' said the old woman, clasping her hands. 'Thank God for that! Thank –'

She broke off suddenly as the sinister meaning of the assurance dawned upon her, and she saw the awful confirmation of her fears in the other's averted face. She caught her breath, and turning to her slower-witted husband, laid her trembling old hand upon his. There was a long silence.

'He was caught in the machinery,' said the visitor at length in a low voice.

'Caught in the machinery,' repeated Mr White in a dazed fashion, 'yes.'

He sat staring blankly out at the window, and taking his wife's hand between his own, pressed it as he had been wont to do in their old courting days nearly forty years before.

'He was the only one left to us,' he said, turning gently to the visitor. 'It is hard.'

The other coughed, and rising, walked slowly to the window. 'The firm wished me to convey their sincere sympathy with you in your great loss,' he said without looking around. 'I beg that you will understand I am only their servant and merely obeying orders.'

There was no reply; the old woman's face was white, her eyes staring, and her breath inaudible; and on the husband's face was a look such as his friend the sergeant might have carried into his first action.

'I was to say that Maw and Meggins disclaim all responsibility,' continued the other. 'They admit no liability at all, but in consideration of your son's services, they wish to present you with a certain sum as compensation.'

Mr White dropped his wife's hand, and rising to his feet, gazed with a look of horror at his visitor. His dry lips shaped the words, 'How much?'

'Two hundred pounds,' was the answer.

Unconscious of his wife's shriek, the old man smiled faintly, put out his hands like a sightless man, and dropped, a senseless heap, to the floor.

In the huge new cemetery, some miles distant, the old people buried their dead, and came back to a house steeped in shadow and silence. It was all over so quickly that at first they could hardly realize it, and remained in a state of expectation as though of something else to happen – something else which was to lighten this load, too heavy for old hearts to bear.

But the days passed, and expectation gave place to **resignation** – the hopeless resignation of the old, sometimes miscalled **apathy**. Sometimes, they hardly exchanged a word, for now they had nothing to talk about, and their days were long to weariness.

It was about a week after, that the old man, waking suddenly in the night, stretched out his hand and found himself alone. The room was in darkness, and the sound of subdued weeping came from the window. He raised himself in bed and listened.

'Come back,' he said, tenderly. 'You will be cold.'

'It is colder for my son,' said the old woman, and wept afresh.

The sound of her sobs died away on his ears. The bed was warm, and his eyes heavy with sleep. He dozed

---

resignation: acceptance
apathy: lack of feeling

fitfully and then slept until a sudden wild cry from his wife awoke him with a start.

'*The paw!*' she cried wildly. 'The monkey's paw!'

He started up in alarm. 'Where? Where is it? What's the matter?'

She came stumbling across the room towards him. 'I want it,' she said quietly. 'You've not destroyed it?'

'It's in the parlour, on the bracket,' he replied, marvelling. 'Why?'

She cried and laughed together, and bending over, kissed his cheek.

'I only just thought of it,' she said, hysterically. 'Why didn't I think of it before? Why didn't you think of it?'

'Think of what?' he questioned.

'The other two wishes,' she replied, rapidly. 'We've only had one.'

'Was not that enough?' he demanded fiercely.

'No,' she cried triumphantly; 'we'll have one more. Go down and get it quickly, and wish our boy alive again.'

The man sat up in bed and flung the bedclothes from his quaking limbs. 'Good God, you are mad!' he cried aghast.

'Get it,' she panted, 'get it quickly, and wish – Oh, my boy, my boy!'

Her husband struck a match and lit the candle. 'Get back to bed,' he said unsteadily. 'You don't know what you are saying.'

'We had the first wish granted,' said the old woman, feverishly; 'why not the second?'

'A coincidence,' stammered the old man.

'Go and get it and wish,' cried his wife, quivering with excitement.

The old man turned and regarded her, and his voice shook. 'He has been dead ten days, and besides he – I would not tell you else, but – I could only recognize him by his clothing. If he was too terrible for you to see then, how now?'

'Bring him back,' cried the old woman, and dragged him towards the door. 'Do you think I fear the child I have nursed?'

He went down in the darkness, and felt his way to the parlour, and then to the mantelpiece. The talisman was in its place, and a horrible fear that the unspoken wish might bring his mutilated son before him ere he could escape from the room seized upon him, and he caught his breath as he found that he had lost the direction of the door. His brow cold with sweat, he felt his way round the table, and groped along the wall until he found himself in the small passage with the unwholesome thing in his hand.

Even his wife's face seemed changed as he entered the room. It was white and expectant, and to his fears seemed to have an unnatural look upon it. He was afraid of her.

'*Wish*,' she cried in a strong voice.

'It is foolish and wicked,' he faltered.

'*Wish!*' repeated his wife.

He raised his hand. 'I wish my son alive again.'

The talisman fell to the floor, and he regarded it fearfully. Then he sank trembling into a chair as the old woman, with burning eyes, walked to the window and raised the blind.

He sat until he was chilled with the cold, glancing occasionally at the figure of the old woman peering through the window. The candle-end, which had burned below the rim of the china candlestick, was throwing pulsating shadows on the ceiling and walls, until, with a flicker larger than the rest, it expired. The old man, with an unspeakable sense of relief at the failure of the talisman, crept back to his bed, and a minute or two afterwards the old woman came silently and apathetically beside him.

Neither spoke, but lay silently listening to the ticking of the clock. A stair creaked, and a squeaky mouse scurried noisily through the wall. The darkness was oppressive, and after lying for some time, screwing up his courage, he took the box of matches, and striking one, went downstairs for a candle.

At the foot of the stairs the match went out, and he paused to strike another; and at the same moment a knock, so quiet and stealthy as to be scarcely audible, sounded on the front door.

The matches fell from his hand and spilled in the passage. He stood motionless, his breath suspended until the knock was repeated. Then he turned and fled swiftly back to his room, and closed the door behind him. A third knock sounded through the house.

'*What's that?*' cried the old woman, starting up.

'A rat,' said the old man in shaking tones, '– a rat. It passed me on the stairs.'

His wife sat up in bed listening. A loud knock resounded through the house.

'It's Herbert!' she screamed. 'It's Herbert!'

She ran to the door, but her husband was before her, and catching her by the arm, held her tightly.

'What are you going to do?' he whispered hoarsely.

'It's my boy; it's Herbert!' she cried, struggling mechanically. 'I forgot it was two miles away. What are you holding me for? Let go. I must open the door.'

'For God's sake don't let it in,' cried the old man, trembling.

'You're afraid of your own son,' she cried, struggling. 'Let me go. I'm coming, Herbert; I'm coming.'

There was another knock, and another. The old woman with a sudden wrench broke free and ran from the room. Her husband followed to the landing, and called after her appealingly as she hurried downstairs. He heard the chain rattle back and the bottom bolt drawn slowly and stiffly from the socket. Then the old woman's voice, strained and panting.

'The bolt,' she cried loudly. 'Come down. I can't reach it.'

But her husband was on his hands and knees groping wildly on the floor in search of the paw. If he could only find it before the thing outside got in. A perfect **fusillade** of knocks reverberated through the house, and he heard the scraping of a chair as his wife put it down in the passage against the door. He heard the creaking of the bolt as it came slowly back, and at the same moment he found the monkey's paw, and frantically breathed his third and last wish.

The knocking ceased suddenly, although the echoes of it were still in the house. He heard the chair drawn back, and the door opened. A cold wind rushed up the staircase, and a long loud wail of disappointment and misery from his wife gave him the courage to run down to her side, and then to the gate beyond. The street lamp flickering opposite shone on a quiet and deserted road.

---

fusillade: continuous outburst

Napoleon and the Spectre
Charlotte Brontë, 1816–1855

When Charlotte Brontë was small, her father brought home a box of toy soldiers. She and her sisters invented characters for their favourites and wrote about their adventures in imaginary lands. Charlotte was also drawn to the real-life soldiers of the time, Napoleon and his conqueror Wellington. It is not surprising that one of her first complete stories was about Napoleon Bonaparte, written after his death.

When a ghost visits Napoleon Bonaparte one night, it forces him to accompany it on a frightening journey in which Bonaparte needs all his courage and determination . . .

Well, as I was saying, the Emperor got into bed.

'Chevalier,' says he to his **valet**, 'let down those window-curtains, and shut the **casement** before you leave the room.'

Chevalier did as he was told, and then, taking up his candlestick, departed.

In a few minutes the Emperor felt his pillow becoming rather hard, and he got up to shake it. As he did so a slight rustling noise was heard near the bed-head. His Majesty listened, but all was silent as he lay down again.

Scarcely had he settled into a peaceful attitude of **repose**, when he was disturbed by a sensation of thirst. Lifting himself on his elbow, he took a glass of lemonade from the small stand which was placed beside him. He refreshed himself by a deep draught. As he returned the goblet to its station a deep groan burst from a kind of closet in one corner of the apartment.

'Who's there?' cried the Emperor, seizing his pistols. 'Speak, or I'll blow your brains out.'

This threat produced no other effect than a short, sharp laugh, and a dead silence followed.

The Emperor started from his couch, and, hastily throwing on a *robe-de-chambre* which hung over the back of a chair, stepped courageously to the haunted closet. As he opened the door something rustled. He sprang forward, sword in hand. No soul or even substance appeared, and the rustling, it was evident, proceeded from the falling of a cloak, which had been suspended by a peg from the door.

Half ashamed of himself he returned to bed.

Just as he was about once more to close his eyes, the light of the three wax tapers, which burned in a silver branch over the mantelpiece, was suddenly darkened. He looked up. A black, **opaque** shadow obscured it. Sweating with terror, the Emperor put out his hand to seize the **bell-rope**, but some invisible being snatched it rudely from his grasp, and at the same instant the **ominous** shade vanished.

'Pooh!' exclaimed Napoleon, 'it was but an **ocular delusion**.'

---

valet: manservant

casement: window

repose: rest

robe-de-chambre: dressing gown

opaque: obscure, dark

bell-rope: rope which rings a bell for assistance

ominous: evil

ocular delusion: imaginary vision

'Who's there?' cried the Emperor, seizing his pistols

'Was it?' whispered a hollow voice, in deep mysterious tones, close to his ear. 'Was it a delusion, Emperor of France? No! all thou hast heard and seen is sad forewarning reality. Rise, lifter of the Eagle Standard! Awake, swayer of the Lily Sceptre! Follow me, Napoleon, and thou shalt see more.'

As the voice ceased, a form dawned on his astonished sight. It was that of a tall, thin man, dressed in a blue **surtout** edged with gold lace. It wore a black **cravat** very tightly round its neck, and confined by two little sticks placed behind each ear. The **countenance** was **livid**; the tongue protruded from between the teeth, and the eyes all glazed and bloodshot started with frightful prominence from their sockets.

'*Mon Dieu!*' exclaimed the Emperor, 'what do I see? Spectre, whence cometh thou?'

The apparition spoke not, but gliding forward beckoned Napoleon with uplifted finger to follow.

Controlled by a mysterious influence, which deprived him of the capability of either thinking or acting for himself, he obeyed in silence.

The solid wall of the apartment fell open as they approached, and, when both had passed through, it closed behind them with a noise like thunder.

They would now have been in total darkness had it not been for a dim light which shone round the ghost and revealed the damp walls of a long, vaulted passage. Down this they proceeded with mute rapidity. Ere long

---

surtout: overcoat
cravat: necktie, scarf
countenance: facial expression
livid: discoloured

a cool, refreshing breeze, which rushed wailing up the **vault** and caused the Emperor to wrap his loose nightdress closer round, announced their approach to the open air.

This they soon reached, and Nap found himself in one of the principal streets of Paris.

'Worthy Spirit,' said he, shivering in the chill night air, 'permit me to return and put on some additional clothing. I will be with you again presently.'

'Forward,' replied his companion sternly.

He felt compelled, in spite of the rising indignation which almost choked him, to obey.

On they went through the deserted streets till they arrived at a lofty house built on the banks of the Seine. Here the Spectre stopped, the gates rolled back to receive them, and they entered a large marble hall which was partly concealed by a curtain drawn across, through the half transparent folds of which a bright light might be seen burning with dazzling lustre. A row of fine female figures, richly attired, stood before this screen. They wore on their heads garlands of the most beautiful flowers, but their faces were concealed by ghastly masks representing **death's-heads**.

'What is all this **mummery**?' cried the Emperor, making an effort to shake off the mental shackles by which he was so unwillingly restrained, 'Where am I, and why have I been brought here?'

'Silence,' said the guide, lolling out still further his black and bloody tongue. 'Silence, if thou wouldst escape instant death.'

The Emperor would have replied, his natural courage overcoming the temporary awe to which he had at first been subjected, but just then a strain of wild, supernatural music swelled behind the huge curtain, which waved to and fro, and bellied slowly out as if agitated by some internal commotion or battle of waving winds. At the same moment an overpowering mixture of the scents of **mortal corruption**, blent with the richest Eastern odours, stole through the haunted hall.

A murmur of many voices was now heard at a distance, and something grasped his arm eagerly from behind.

He turned hastily round. His eyes met the well-known countenance of Marie Louise.

'What! are you in this infernal place, too?' said he. 'What has brought you here?'

'Will your Majesty permit me to ask the same question of yourself?' said the Empress, smiling.

He made no reply; astonishment prevented him.

No curtain now intervened between him and the light. It had been removed as if by magic, and a splendid chandelier appeared suspended over his head. Throngs of ladies, richly dressed, but without death's-head masks, stood round, and a due proportion of gay cavaliers was mingled with them. Music was still sounding, but it was seen to proceed from a band of mortal musicians stationed in an orchestra near at hand. The air was yet **redolent** of incense, but it was incense unblended with stench.

'*Mon Dieu!*' cried the Emperor, 'how is all this come

---

vault: arched roof
death's-heads: skulls
mummery: performance, foolishness
mortal corruption: rotting flesh
redolent: smelling

about? Where in the world is **Piche**?'

'Piche?' replied the Empress. 'What does your Majesty mean? Had you not better leave the apartment and retire to rest?'

'Leave the apartment? Why, where am I?'

'In my private drawing-room, surrounded by a few particular persons of the Court whom I had invited this evening to a ball. You entered a few minutes since in your nightdress with your eyes fixed and wide open. I suppose from the astonishment you now **testify** that you were walking in your sleep.'

The Emperor immediately fell into a fit of **catalepsy**, in which he continued during the whole of that night and the greater part of the next day.

Piche: the spectre's name. Charlotte Brontë believed that Napoleon had ordered the murder of a French General called Pichegru, so it may be no coincidence that Piche is the name of the spectre

testify: declare

catalepsy: trance-like state

The Signalman

Charles Dickens, 1812–1879

Maybe Dickens' love of chilling tales such as The Signalman *and* A Christmas Carol *began when he was a child. His nurse would tell him ghoulish tales of the supernatural and pass on horrors told her by the midwife and undertaker. Dickens combined these early experiences with the corresponding development of railway travel as passengers were always ready to read of mysterious happenings concerning trains.*

In his signal-box by a gloomy railway cutting with its dark tunnel the signalman is haunted by mysterious events which fill him with foreboding and fear . . .

'Halloa! Below there!'

When he heard a voice thus calling to him, he was standing at the door of his box, with a flag in his hand, furled round its short pole. One would have thought, considering the nature of the ground, that he could not have doubted from what quarter the voice came; but instead of looking up to where I stood on the top of the steep cutting nearly over his head, he turned himself about, and looked down the Line. There was something remarkable in his manner of doing so, though I could not have said for my life what. But I know it was remarkable enough to attract my notice, even though his figure was foreshortened and shadowed, down in the deep trench, and mine was high above him, so steeped in the glow of an angry sunset, that I had shaded my eyes with my hand before I saw him at all.

'Halloa! Below!'

From looking down the Line, he turned himself about again, and, raising his eyes, saw my figure high above him.

'Is there any path by which I can come down and speak to you?'

He looked up at me without replying, and I looked down at him without pressing him too soon with a repetition of my idle question. Just then there came a vague vibration in the earth and air, quickly changing into a violent pulsation, and an oncoming rush that caused me to start back, as though it had force to draw me down. When such vapour as rose to my height from this rapid train had passed me, and was skimming away over the landscape, I looked down again, and saw him refurling the flag he had shown while the train went by.

I repeated my inquiry. After a pause, during which he seemed to regard me with fixed attention, he motioned with his rolled-up flag towards a point on my level, some two or three hundred yards distant. I called down to him, 'All right!' and made for that point. There, by dint of looking closely about me, I found a rough zigzag descending path notched out, which I followed.

The cutting was extremely deep, and unusually **precipitate**. It was made through a clammy stone, that became oozier and wetter as I went down. For these reasons, I found the way long enough to give me time to recall a singular air of reluctance or compulsion with which he had pointed out the path.

When I came down low enough upon the zigzag descent to see him again, I saw that he was standing between the rails on the way by which the train had lately passed, in an attitude as if he were waiting for me to appear. He had his left hand at his chin, and that left elbow rested on his right hand, crossed over his breast. His attitude was one of such expectation and watchfulness that I stopped a moment, wondering at it.

I resumed my downward way, and stepping out upon the level of the railroad, and drawing nearer to him, saw that he was a dark sallow man, with a dark beard and rather heavy eyebrows. His post was in as solitary and dismal a place as ever I saw. On either side, a dripping-wet wall of jagged stone, excluding all view but a strip of sky; the perspective one way only a crooked prolongation of this great dungeon; the shorter perspective in the other direction **terminating** in a gloomy red light, and the gloomier entrance to a black tunnel, in whose massive architecture there was a **barbarous**, depressing, and forbidding air. So little sunlight ever found its way to this spot, that it had an earthy, deadly smell; and so much cold wind rushed through it, that it struck chill to me, as if I had left the natural world.

Before he stirred, I was near enough to him to have touched him. Not even then removing his eyes from mine, he stepped back one step, and lifted his hand.

This was a lonesome post to occupy (I said), and it had riveted my attention when I looked down from up yonder. A visitor was a rarity, I should suppose; not an unwelcome rarity, I hoped? In me, he merely saw a man who had been shut up within narrow limits all his life, and who, being at last set free, had a newly-awakened interest in these great works. To

---

precipitate: steep
terminating: ending
barbarous: rough

His attitude was one of such expectation and watchfulness that I stopped a moment, wondering at it

such purpose I spoke to him; but I am far from sure of the terms I used; for, besides that I am not happy in opening any conversation, there was something in the man that daunted me.

He directed a most curious look towards the red light near the tunnel's mouth, and looked all about it, as if something were missing from it, and then looked at me.

That light was part of his charge? Was it not?

He answered in a low voice, – 'Don't you know it is?'

The monstrous thought came into my mind, as I **perused** the fixed eyes and the **saturnine** face, that this was a spirit, not a man. I have speculated since, whether there may have been infection in his mind.

In my turn, I stepped back. But in making the action, I detected in his eyes some latent fear of me. This put the monstrous thought to flight.

'You look at me,' I said, forcing a smile, 'as if you had a dread of me.'

'I was doubtful,' he returned, 'whether I had seen you before.'

'Where?'

He pointed to the red light he had looked at.

'There?' I said.

Intently watchful of me, he replied (but without sound), 'Yes.'

'My good fellow, what should I do there? However, be that as it may, I never was there, you may swear.'

'I think I may,' he rejoined. 'Yes; I am sure I may.'

His manner cleared, like my own. He replied to my remarks with readiness, and in well-chosen words.

---

perused: examined carefully
saturnine: gloomy

Charles Dickens

Had he much to do there? Yes; that was to say, he had enough responsibility to bear; but exactness and watchfulness were what was required of him, and of actual work – manual labour – he had next to none. To change that signal, to trim those lights, and to turn this iron handle now and then, was all he had to do under that head. Regarding those many long and lonely hours of which I seemed to make so much, he could only say that the routine of his life had shaped itself into that form, and he had grown used to it. He had taught himself a language down here, – if only to know it by sight, and to have formed his own crude ideas of its pronunciation, could be called learning it. He had also worked at fractions and decimals, and tried a little algebra; but he was, and had been as a boy, a poor hand at figures. Was it necessary for him when on duty always to remain in that channel of damp air, and could he never rise into the sunshine from between those high stone walls? Why, that depended upon times and circumstances. Under some conditions there would be less upon the Line than under others, and the same held good as to certain hours of the day and night. In bright weather, he did choose occasions for getting a little above these lower shadows; but, being at all times liable to be called by his electric bell, and at such times listening for it with redoubled anxiety, the relief was less than I would suppose.

He took me into his box, where there was a fire, a desk for an official book in which he had to make certain entries, a telegraphic instrument with its dial, face, and needles, and the little bell of which he had spoken. On my trusting that he would excuse the remark that he had been well educated, and (I hoped I might say without offence), perhaps educated above that station, he observed that instances of slight

incongruity in such wise would rarely be found wanting among large bodies of men; that he had heard it was so in workhouses, in the police force, even in that last desperate resource, the army; and that he knew it was so, more or less, in any great railway staff. He had been, when young (if I could believe it, sitting in that hut, – he scarcely could), a student of natural philosophy, and had attended lectures; but he had run wild, misused his opportunities, gone down, and never risen again. He had no complaint to offer about that. He had made his bed, and he lay upon it. It was far too late to make another.

All that I have here **condensed** he said in a quiet manner, with his grave dark regards divided between me and the fire. He threw in the word, 'Sir,' from time to time, and especially when he referred to his youth, – as though to request me to understand that he claimed to be nothing but what I found him. He was several times interrupted by the little bell, and had to read off messages, and send replies. Once he had to stand without the door, and display a flag as a train passed, and make some verbal communication to the driver. In the discharge of his duties, I observed him to be remarkably exact and vigilant, breaking off his discourse at a syllable, and remaining silent until what he had to do was done.

In a word, I should have set this man down as one of the safest of men to be employed in that capacity, but for the circumstance that while he was speaking to me he twice broke off with a fallen colour, turned his face towards the little bell when it did NOT ring, opened the

---

incongruity: out of keeping
condensed: shortened

door of the hut (which was kept shut to exclude the unhealthy damp), and looked out towards the red light near the mouth of the tunnel. On both of those occasions, he came back to the fire with the inexplicable air upon him which I had remarked, without being able to define, when we were so far **asunder**.

Said I, when I rose to leave him, 'You almost make me think that I have met with a contented man.'

(I am afraid I must acknowledge that I said it to lead him on.)

'I believe I used to be so,' he rejoined, in the low voice in which he had first spoken; 'but I am troubled, sir, I am troubled.'

He would have recalled the words if he could. He had said them, however, and I took them up quickly.

'With what? What is your trouble?'

'It is very difficult to impart, sir. It is very, very difficult to speak of. If ever you make me another visit, I will try to tell you.'

'But I expressly intend to make you another visit. Say, when shall it be?'

'I go off early in the morning, and I shall be on again at ten to-morrow night, sir.'

'I will come at eleven.'

He thanked me, and went out at the door with me. 'I'll show my white light, sir,' he said, in his peculiar low voice, 'till you have found the way up. When you have found it, don't call out! And when you are at the top, don't call out!'

His manner seemed to make the place strike colder to me, but I said no more than, 'Very well.'

'And when you come down to-morrow night, don't call out! Let me ask you a parting question. What made you cry, "Halloa! Below there!" to-night?'

'Heaven knows,' said I. 'I cried something to that effect –'

'Not to that effect, sir. Those were the very words. I know them well.'

'Admit those were the very words. I said them, no doubt, because I saw you below.'

'For no other reason?'

'What other reason could I possibly have?'

'You had no feeling that they were conveyed to you in any supernatural way?'

'No.'

He wished me good night, and held up his light. I walked by the side of the down Line of rails (with a very disagreeable sensation of a train coming behind me) until I found the path. It was easier to mount than to descend, and I got back to my inn without any adventure.

Punctual to my appointment, I placed my foot on the first notch of the zigzag next night, as the distant clocks were striking eleven. He was waiting for me at the bottom, with his white light on. 'I have not called out,' I said, when we came close together; 'may I speak now?' 'By all means, sir.' 'Good night, then, and here's my hand.' 'Good night, sir, and here's mine.' With that we walked side by side to his box, entered it, closed the door, and sat down by the fire.

'I have made up my mind, sir,' he began, bending forward as soon as we were seated, and speaking in a tone but a little above a whisper, 'that you shall not have to ask me twice what troubles me. I took you for some one else yesterday evening. That troubles me.'

'That mistake?'

---

asunder: apart

'No. That some one else.'

'Who is it?'

'I don't know.'

'Like me?'

'I don't know. I never saw the face. The left arm is across the face, and the right arm is waved, – violently waved. This way.'

I followed his action with my eyes, and it was the action of an arm gesticulating, with the utmost passion and **vehemence**, 'For God's sake, clear the way!'

'One moonlight night,' said the man, 'I was sitting here, when I heard a voice cry, "Halloa! Below there!" I started up, looked from that door, and saw this Some one else standing by the red light near the tunnel, waving as I just now showed you. The voice seemed hoarse with shouting, and it cried, "Look out! Look out!" And then again, "Halloa! Below there! Look out!" I caught up my lamp, turned it on red, and ran towards the figure, calling, "What's wrong? What has happened? Where?" It stood just outside the blackness of the tunnel. I advanced so close upon it that I wondered at its keeping the sleeve across its eyes. I ran right up at it, and had my hand stretched out to pull the sleeve away, when it was gone.'

'Into the tunnel?' said I.

'No. I ran on into the tunnel, five hundred yards. I stopped, and held my lamp above my head, and saw the figures of the measured distance, and saw the wet stains stealing down the walls and trickling through the arch. I ran out again faster than I had run in (for I had a mortal **abhorrence** of the place upon me), and I looked all round the red light with my own red light, and I went up the iron ladder to the gallery atop of it, and I came down again, and ran back here. I telegraphed both ways, "An alarm has been given. Is anything wrong?" The answer came back, both ways, "All well."'

Resisting the slow touch of a frozen finger tracing out my spine, I showed him how that this figure must be a deception of his sense of sight; and how that figures, originating in disease of the delicate nerves that minister to the functions of the eye, were known to have often troubled patients, some of whom had become conscious of the nature of their affliction, and had even proved it by experiments upon themselves. 'As to an imaginary cry,' said I, 'do but listen for a moment to the wind in this unnatural valley while we speak so low, and to the wild harp it makes of the telegraph wires.'

That was all very well, he returned, after we had sat listening for a while, and he ought to know something of the wind and the wires, – he who so often passed long winter nights there, alone and watching. But he would beg to remark that he had not finished.

I asked his pardon, and he slowly added these words, touching my arm, –

'Within six hours after the Appearance, the memorable accident on this Line happened, and within ten hours the dead and wounded were brought along through the tunnel over the spot where the figure had stood.'

A disagreeable shudder crept over me, but I did my best against it. It was not to be denied, I rejoined, that this was a remarkable coincidence, calculated deeply to impress his mind. But it was unquestionable that

---

vehemence: energy
abhorrence: hatred

remarkable coincidences did continually occur, and they must be taken into account in dealing with such a subject. Though to be sure I must admit, I added (for I thought I saw that he was going to bring the objection to bear upon me), men of common sense did not allow much for coincidences in making the ordinary calculations of life.

He again begged to remark that he had not finished.

I again begged his pardon for being betrayed into interruptions.

'This,' he said, again laying his hand upon my arm, and glancing over his shoulder with hollow eyes, 'was just a year ago. Six or seven months passed, and I had recovered from the surprise and shock, when one morning, as the day was breaking, I, standing at the door, looked towards the red light, and saw the spectre again.' He stopped, with a fixed look at me.

'Did it cry out?'

'No. It was silent.'

'Did it wave its arm?'

'No. It leaned against the shaft of the light, with both hands before the face. Like this.'

Once more I followed his action with my eyes. It was an action of mourning. I have seen such an attitude in stone figures on tombs.

'Did you go up to it?'

'I came in and sat down, partly to collect my thoughts, partly because it had turned me faint. When I went to the door again, daylight was above me, and the ghost was gone.'

'But nothing followed? Nothing came of this?'

He touched me on the arm with his forefinger twice or thrice, giving a ghastly nod each time:

'That very day, as a train came out of the tunnel, I noticed, at a carriage window on my side, what looked like a confusion of hands and heads, and something waved. I saw it just in time to signal the driver, Stop! He shut off, and put his brake on, but the train drifted past here a hundred and fifty yards or more. I ran after it, and, as I went along, heard terrible screams and cries. A beautiful young lady had died instantaneously in one of the compartments, and was brought in here, and laid down on this floor between us.'

Involuntarily I pushed my chair back, as I looked from the boards at which he pointed to himself.

'True, sir. True. Precisely as it happened, so I tell it you.'

I could think of nothing to say, to any purpose, and my mouth was very dry. The wind and the wires took up the story with a long lamenting wail.

He resumed. 'Now, sir, mark this, and judge how my mind is troubled. The spectre came back a week ago. Ever since, it has been there, now and again, by fits and starts.'

'At the light?'

'At the Danger-light.'

'What does it seem to do?'

He repeated, if possible with increased passion and vehemence, that former gesticulation of, 'For God's sake, clear the way!'

Then he went on. 'I have no peace or rest for it. It calls to me, for many minutes together, in an agonised manner, "Below there! Look out! Look out!" It stands waving to me. It rings my little bell –'

I caught at that. 'Did it ring your bell yesterday evening when I was here, and you went to the door?'

'Twice.'

'Why, see,' said I, 'how your imagination misleads you. My eyes were on the bell, and my ears were open to the bell, and if I am a living man, it did NOT ring at those times. No, nor at any other time, except when it was rung in the natural course of physical things by the station communicating with you.'

He shook his head. 'I have never made a mistake as to that yet, sir. I have never confused the spectre's ring with the man's. The ghost's ring is a strange vibration in the bell that it derives from nothing else, and I have not asserted that the bell stirs to the eye. I don't wonder that you failed to hear it. But *I* heard it.'

'And did the spectre seem to be there, when you looked out?'

'It WAS there.'

'Both times?'

He repeated firmly: 'Both times.'

'Will you come to the door with me, and look for it now?'

He bit his under lip as though he were somewhat unwilling, but arose. I opened the door, and stood on the step, while he stood in the doorway. There was the Danger-light. There was the dismal mouth of the tunnel. There were the high, wet stone walls of the cutting. There were the stars above them.

'Do you see it?' I asked him, taking particular note of his face. His eyes were prominent and strained, but not very much more so, perhaps, than my own had been when I had directed them earnestly towards the same spot.

'No,' he answered. 'It is not there.'

'Agreed,' said I.

We went in again, shut the door, and resumed our seats. I was thinking how best to improve this advantage, if it might be called one, when he took up the conversation in such a matter-of-course way, so assuming that there could be no serious question of fact between us, that I felt myself placed in the weakest of positions.

'By this time you will fully understand, sir,' he said, 'that what troubles me so dreadfully is the question, What does the spectre mean?'

I was not sure, I told him, that I did fully understand.

'What is its warning against?' he said, **ruminating**, with his eyes on the fire, and only by times turning them on me. 'What is the danger? Where is the danger? There is danger over-hanging somewhere on the Line. Some dreadful calamity will happen. It is not to be doubted this third time, after what has gone before. But surely this is a cruel haunting of *me*. What can *I* do?'

He pulled out his handkerchief, and wiped the drops from his heated forehead.

'If I telegraph Danger, on either side of me, or on both, I can give no reason for it,' he went on, wiping the palms of his hands. 'I should get into trouble, and do no good. They would think I was mad. This is the way it would work, – Message: "Danger! Take care!" Answer: "What Danger? Where?" Message: "Don't know. But, for God's sake, take care!" They would displace me. What else could they do?'

His pain of mind was most pitiable to see. It was the mental torture of a conscientious man, **oppressed beyond endurance** by an unintelligible responsibility involving life.

'When it first stood under the Danger-light,' he went on, putting his dark hair back from his head, and

---

ruminating: thinking
oppressed beyond endurance: pushed too far

drawing his hands outward across and across his temples in an extremity of feverish distress, 'why not tell me where that accident was to happen, – if it must happen? Why not tell me how it could be averted, – if it could have been averted? When on its second coming it hid its face, why not tell me, instead, "She is going to die. Let them keep her at home"? If it came, on those two occasions, only to show me that its warnings were true, and so to prepare me for the third, why not warn me plainly now? And I, Lord help me! A mere poor signalman on this solitary station! Why not go to somebody with credit to be believed, and power to act?'

When I saw him in this state, I saw that for the poor man's sake, as well as for the public safety, what I had to do for the time was to compose his mind. Therefore, setting aside all question of reality or unreality between us, I represented to him that whoever thoroughly discharged his duty must do well, and that at least it was his comfort that he understood his duty, though he did not understand these confounding Appearances. In this effort I succeeded far better than in the attempt to reason him out of his **conviction**. He became calm; the occupations incidental to his post as the night advanced began to make larger demands on his attention: and I left him at two in the morning. I had offered to stay through the night, but he would not hear of it.

That I more than once looked back at the red light as I ascended the pathway, that I did not like the red light, and that I should have slept but poorly if my bed had been under it, I see no reason to conceal. Nor did I like the two sequences of the accident and the dead girl. I see no reason to conceal that either.

But what ran most in my thoughts was the consideration how ought I to act, having become the recipient of this disclosure? I had proved the man to be intelligent, vigilant, painstaking, and exact; but how long might he remain so, in his state of mind? Though in a subordinate position, still he held a most important trust, and would I (for instance) like to stake my own life on the chances of his continuing to execute it with precision?

Unable to overcome a feeling that there would be something treacherous in my communicating what he had told me to his superiors in the Company, without first being plain with himself and proposing a middle course to him, I ultimately resolved to offer to accompany him (otherwise keeping his secret for the present) to the wisest medical practitioner we could hear of in those parts, and to take his opinion. A change in his time of duty would come round next night, he had **apprised** me, and he would be off an hour or two after sunrise, and on again soon after sunset. I had appointed to return accordingly.

Next evening was a lovely evening, and I walked out early to enjoy it. The sun was not yet quite down when I **traversed** the field-path near the top of the deep cutting. I would extend my walk for an hour, I said to myself, half an hour on and half an hour back, and it would then be time to go to my signalman's box.

Before pursuing my stroll, I stepped to the brink, and mechanically looked down, from the point from which I had first seen him. I cannot describe the thrill that seized upon me, when, close at the mouth of the tunnel, I saw the appearance of a man, with his left

---

conviction: belief
apprised: informed
traversed: walked across

sleeve across his eyes, passionately waving his right arm.

The nameless horror that oppressed me passed in a moment, for in a moment I saw that this appearance of a man was a man indeed, and that there was a little group of other men, standing at a short distance, to whom he seemed to be rehearsing the gesture he made. The Danger-light was not yet lighted. Against its shaft, a little low hut, entirely new to me, had been made of some wooden supports and tarpaulin. It looked no bigger than a bed.

With an irresistible sense that something was wrong, – with a flashing self-reproachful fear that fatal mischief had come of my leaving the man there, and causing no one to be sent to overlook or correct what he did, – I descended the notched path with all the speed I could make.

'What is the matter?' I asked the men.

'Signalman killed this morning, sir.'

'Not the man belonging to that box?'

'Yes, sir.'

'Not the man I know?'

'You will recognize him, sir, if you knew him,' said the man who spoke for the others, solemnly uncovering his own head, and raising an end of the tarpaulin, 'for his face is quite composed.'

'O, how did this happen, how did this happen?' I asked, turning from one to another as the hut closed in again.

'He was cut down by an engine, sir. No man in England knew his work better. But somehow he was not clear of the outer rail. It was just at broad day. He had struck the light, and had the lamp in his hand. As the engine came out of the tunnel, his back was towards her, and she cut him down. That man drove her, and was showing how it happened. Show the gentleman, Tom.'

The man, who wore a rough dark dress, stepped back to his former place at the mouth of the tunnel.

'Coming round the curve in the tunnel, sir,' he said, 'I saw him at the end, like as if I saw him down a **perspective-glass**. There was no time to check speed, and I knew him to be very careful. As he didn't seem to take heed of the whistle, I shut it off when we were running down upon him, and called to him as loud as I could call.'

'What did you say?'

'I said, "Below there! Look out! Look out! For God's sake, clear the way!"'

I started.

'Ah! it was a dreadful time, sir. I never left off calling to him. I put this arm before my eyes not to see, and I waved this arm to the last; but it was no use.'

Without prolonging the narrative to dwell on any one of its curious circumstances more than on any other, I may, in closing it, point out the coincidence that the warning of the engine-driver included, not only the words which the unfortunate signalman had repeated to me as haunting him, but also the words which I myself – not he – had attached, and that only in my own mind, to the gesticulation he had imitated.

---

perspective-glass: telescope

EXPLORATIONS AND ACTIVITIES

Activities *which cover a range of responses including a writing assignment for each individual story start on this page.*

Explorations *which can be used for imaginative and empathic responses across the stories start on page 173.*

Coursework *material which can be used for writing and coursework assignments across the stories start on page 177.*

Extension *activities which involve comparisons of the stories in the book with further texts in line with National Curriculum requirements start on page 181.*

The Necklace

1　In *The Necklace* Mathilde was desperate for an elegant piece of jewellery to wear to the ball. Have you ever wanted something really badly, such as something to wear, or a pet, or something for your hobby? If you have, write about it, explaining:

- what it was
- whether you received it
- if so, whether it lived up to your expectations.

If you did not receive it, how did you feel about it at the time? How do you feel about it now?

2　Read the first three paragraphs of the story again.

a) Make a chart like the one opposite. Find examples of how Mathilde thinks and behaves, and place them in column 1. In column 2, place a precise adjective which sums up Mathilde's character based on the evidence in column 1.

Proof	Characteristic
longed for things that could never be (p.2)	dissatisfied

b) Write a character sketch of Mathilde based on the information in the table.

3 Now make a table and write a character sketch for Loisel, as a contrast. You might like to look at:

- his reaction to the invitation
- how he viewed Mathilde
- how he helped resolve the problem of the lost necklace.

Writing assignments

1 Write an explanation about why Mathilde borrowed the necklace and what you think of her suffering as she paid for the replacement. You might consider:

- why she borrowed the necklace
- whether she deserved to suffer
- your feelings towards her as she saved the money
- your feelings towards her at the end of the story
- what you have learned from the story.

2 Write a modern-day version of the story. Replace the necklace with an appropriate possession such as:

- an item of designer wear
- a work of art
- a car.

The Sexton's Hero

1 Before you read the story, get into small groups.

    a) Look up the dictionary definition of the word 'hero' and write it down.

    b) Make a spider plan like the one below, and arrange around the centre all the words you associate with a hero.

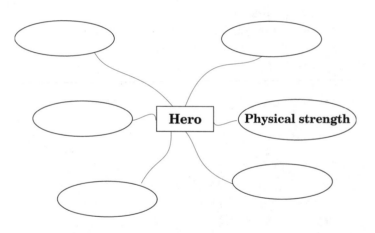

    c) From the words on your plan, select four or five qualities that you think are the most important for a hero to possess.

    d) Choose three people from the past or present whom your group believes to be heroes. Prepare your nominations and reasons, and present your findings to the class.

2   Soon after Gilbert arrived in the village the sexton 'got to hate him' (page 17). Explain why this was so. Look carefully at his physical appearance, skills, personality, intellect, and how he was viewed by those around him.

3   Imagine you were Gilbert's friend at the time he refused to fight the sexton. When he was called a coward, what would have been your advice to him? Write your advice in the form of a letter, or prepare a speech.

Writing assignments

1   Jeremy thought that a hero was someone who carried out their duty and had personal strengths or who fought battles. Explain how Gilbert was shown to be a true hero. You might like to consider:

- physical strength
- character
- beliefs
- actions.

2   Choose three people whom you believe to be heroic. Try to select a person who represents each of the following categories:

- internationally recognized
- nationally known
- a friend or member of your family.

In each case explain the ways in which you feel they are heroic.

The Gift of the Magi

1 You can work out what a character is like by looking at the way they behave, what they say, and how they say it.

    a) Make a table like the one below, then read the story carefully. Find examples of Della's behaviour, what she says and how it is delivered. Record your findings in column 1. On the basis of the evidence you have found, think of adjectives which sum up Della's character and place them in column 2.

Evidence	Characteristic
howls (p.30)	emotional
gives an ecstatic scream (p.37)	
produces 'hysterical tears' (p.37)	

    b) Using the evidence you have collected in your table write a character sketch of Della, selecting the best examples for each characteristic.

2 Explain in your own words why Della and Jim were 'magi'. The last paragraph may help you.

Writing assignments

1 The story is written from Della's point of view. Imagine you are Jim and write your diary entry for Christmas Eve. Remember to include:

- your efforts to choose and buy a gift for Della
- your reaction to her gift
- thoughts and feelings about the event
- plans for the next couple of days.

2 Imagine you are the hairdresser Della visited. Write a letter to a friend describing Della's visit. You might like to include:

- actions and events prior to Della's arrival
- your reaction to her entrance and request
- your thoughts and feelings about her decision and her reason for it.

3 Della and Jim both 'sacrifice for each other the greatest treasures of their house' (page 38). Write about your most treasured possession, describing it carefully. Explain how it came to be yours and why it is so treasured. Remember that 'valuable' is not always the same as 'expensive'.

Extension

Research the stories of famous lovers, real and fictional, such as Romeo and Juliet, or Heloise and Abelard.

- Did they make sacrifices for each other?
- How did their lives turn out?

The Parvenue

1 In *The Parvenue* the narrator, Fanny, experienced difficulties because she married someone of greater wealth and a more important background than herself. This meant that her husband had a great influence on the narrator's life and that of her family. Do you think such a situation could arise today? You might like to consider:

- educational opportunities
- the changing role of women
- equal opportunity laws
- the legal rights of women in relationships
- financial and other support available from social services.

2 After reading the story it is clear that the narrator is an emotional woman. Using a chart like the one below, plot her changing emotional state from childhood, through youth, her courtship and marriage to the time of her emigration. Begin with her idyllic childhood.

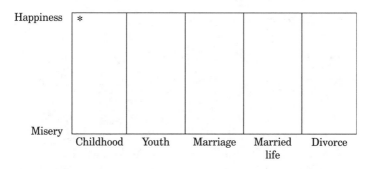

3 In groups of six, each choose a character from the story:

- narrator
- husband
- mother
- sister – Susan
- father
- brother-in-law – Lawrence.

Create a 'freeze-frame' picture of the moment when her husband asked her to 'choose between us' (page 53). The narrator should stand centre-front. The other characters should reflect their relationship with her through their distance from her, body language and facial expressions. Once you have your 'frame', each character should give a brief explanation of their position and feelings to the class.

Writing assignments

1 Imagine you were the narrator's friend at the time she had to choose between her husband and family. Write her a letter in which you:

- sympathize with her situation
- examine her options
- suggest a plan of action.

2 At the time the story was set the narrator, like most other women of the time, would have had no independent means of income or legal claim to her husband's wealth. This made her choice between husband and family all the more difficult. After reading the story carefully and using any knowledge you have of the social history of the time, explain:

- why her decision was difficult
- how her family and husband behaved towards her
- what you think of her decision
- any other choices open to her.

An Alpine Divorce

1 In groups, create a radio news broadcast of the story as if it happened today:

- introduce the programme
- report the story
- include an interview
- suggest future developments.

2 Write the story of Mrs Bodman's death for the front page of a newspaper. Remember to use:

- a suitable headline
- columns, sub-headings and pictures
- an interview with one of the men who found Mr Bodman on the cliff.

3 In groups, 'hotseat' Mr Bodman with an audience questioning him about his wife's death, the events leading up to it, his thoughts and feelings, and his future plans.

4 In groups of three imagine you are Mr and Mrs Bodman, discussing your difficult relationship with a third party such as a mutual friend or a marriage guidance counsellor. Let each party air their grievances and the third person should suggest possible solutions to their problems. Use the information in the story and add any extra details you feel are appropriate.

Writing assignment

Imagine you are Mrs Bodman. Write her diary entry for the day before her death. You might like to include:

- her attitude toward her husband
- her thoughts and feelings, past and present, about her marriage
- her reasons for deciding on suicide.

The Thieves who Couldn't Help Sneezing

1 Imagine you were the leader of the thieves' gang. Write out your plan for the robbery, step by step. Number each stage like an action plan.

2 In groups, devise a television interview with Hubert, Sir Simon and one of his guests on the night of the incident. It could be for a news broadcast or for a chat show. If possible, video your interview and replay it for your class.

3 Imagine you were one of the guests at Sir Simon's house on the night of the incident. Tell your version of events to a friend who was not there, either in the form of a letter or a conversation. You might like to include details about:

- what the evening was like before the incident
- the discovery of Hubert and his tale
- the way the thieves were exposed
- how the evening ended.

4 Hubert arrived home at 'about four o'clock in the morning'. Imagine the scene at his house when he finally appeared. With a partner, work out the conversation he might have had with his father or mother. Think about:

- how they would first react to his arrival
- what they had thought during his absence
- how Hubert would relate his experience
- his parents' reaction to the story.

Act out your conversation for the class.

Writing assignment

Write a newspaper front page story or a magazine article about Hubert's exploits:

- invent names for the people and places, where they are not mentioned
- use an appropriate layout and headline
- use subheadings
- include at least one interview.

The Blue Carbuncle

1 Holmes declares that he can 'infer' a great deal about Mr Henry Baker from looking closely at his hat. What does he mean by 'infer'?

2 Carefully select all that Holmes infers about Mr Baker. Using a table like the one below, try to match each inference with the evidence Holmes has found to prove it.

Inference	Proof
Intelligent	Large hat size

3 Holmes not only replaced Mr Baker's goose, he also offered him the 'feathers, legs, crop and so on'. What was his reason for doing this?

4 How did John Horner react and behave when accused of the theft of the jewel (see page 87)? How could his reactions have indicated both innocence and guilt?

5 Trace the blue carbuncle's journey from the Countess of Morcar to Sherlock Holmes. You could set the journey out in a flowchart like the one on the next page, noting the stages of the gem's journey and the names of the people through whose hands it passed.

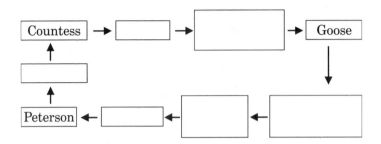

6 Sherlock Holmes did not turn James Ryder over to the police. In your own words explain his reasons for 'commuting a felony'. Do you think he was right to act in this way? Give a reason for your answer.

Writing assignments

1 Choose two or three items such as an article of clothing, a book or a piece of furniture. Use Sherlock Holmes' method of inferring information about the owners. Write an explanation as if you were demonstrating your deduction to a friend or fellow detective.

2 Describe in detail how Sherlock Holmes solved the mystery of the blue carbuncle. You should consider:

- how he inferred important information
- how he used the newspapers
- how he extracted information from people.

The Monkey's Paw

1 Look again at the first part of the story, up to '. . . offhandedly' (page 109). Write down all the clues which make you think the tale will be one of mystery and suspense. Consider:

- the weather
- the time of day
- the atmosphere in the house
- the mood of Mr White
- the topics of conversation.

2 Explain why the Whites' wish seemed like a good idea at the time. Then, in your own words, explain what went wrong with it. Rephrase the Whites' first wish more carefully so it would not bring about the events in the story.

3 What do you think Mr White's third wish was? Write it down in speech marks as if he was wishing aloud.

4 In groups, decide upon three wishes you would make if you had a lucky charm. Try to make your wishes include some consideration towards others, such as your family and friends. Present your ideas to the class.

Writing assignment

The idea of something to grant your wishes may seem very good, but Sergeant-Major Morris does not agree.

a) Look at his comments about the paw on pages 110–11. Make a table like the one below. In column 1 fill in *what* he says about the paw, in column 2 fill in *how* he says it – his general manner.

What is said	How it is said
Spell put on the paw by a fakir (p.110)	Impressively

b) Using the evidence you have collected in the table, write about how the Whites were warned against the paw.

Napoleon and the Spectre

1 Try to remember your most frequent or most recent dream. Make a note of:

   - who was in it
   - where it was set
   - whether any aspects were repeated
   - whether it was good or bad
   - whether it came true.

   In small groups, take it in turns to relate your dream, using clear descriptions and creating a suitable atmosphere. Select the best account from each group to be presented to the class.

2 After an active and often victorious military career, Napoleon Bonaparte was beaten by the Duke of Wellington at Waterloo in 1815 and exiled to the island of St Helena, where he died. With this historical context in mind, what do you think the spectre was trying to show the Emperor in the dream?

3 In groups, write the story in the form of a playscript.

   The scenes
   Write three scenes set in:

   - Napoleon's bedroom
   - the streets of Paris
   - Marie Louise's apartment.

The cast
You will need the following parts:

- Napoleon
- The Valet
- The Spectre
- Marie Louise
- Guests at the ball.

Writing your script

- Use stage directions in brackets to show how a character would behave or speak their lines, for example:

  Napoleon: (*In a threatening voice*) Speak! Or I'll blow your brains out!

- You do not have to use all the speech given in the story.
- You can use your own words as long as the meaning is not changed.

Performing your script
When you have written your script, allocate roles to members of the group, rehearse it and act it out for the class.

Writing assignment

1 Imagine you were one of the guests at Marie Louise's ball. Write a conversation in which you relate the evening's events to your friends who ask questions and comment on your tale.

2 If nightmares such as Napoleon's predict a future outcome, write the nightmares which may be experienced by two of the following:

- a prime minister, president or king
- an Olympic medal hopeful
- a performer such as a magician, actor or musician.

The Signalman

1 Charles Dickens created an air of mystery and unease through the setting and events of his story rather than through the use of gruesome descriptions with which we are more familiar today. Which do you find more frightening, the explicit horror story or the atmospheric, chilling mystery, where details are left to your imagination?

2 When you call out to someone, as the narrator called out to the signalman at the beginning of this story, you expect them to turn and look at you. The signalman, however, 'turned himself about and looked down the Line'. Why did he act in this unusual manner?

3 Dickens wanted to create a mysterious atmosphere to suit his story, so he chose his words and phrases very carefully.

   • Find and write down the words and phrases on pages 130–31 which describe the tunnel and the part of the line patrolled by the signalman.
   • Explain what they mean and why you think they are effective.

4 Before meeting the narrator, the signalman had twice experienced warnings, followed by fatal accidents. In your own words, explain what each warning was and the incident which followed it.

5 On page 143 the signalman is clearly distressed that a third accident might occur and he cannot prevent it. In your own words, explain why he did not report the warning or call for help.

6 The night before the signalman's death the narrator decided on a plan to help him. Explain in your own words what it was.

Writing assignment

1 Imagine you were the railway official who had to write the report of the signalman's death. Use subheadings and make sure you include details such as:

- the place, date and time of the accident
- cause of death
- statement of the train driver
- statement of the narrator.

You will need to invent some details, such as the signalman's name, the place and the driver's name. Try to keep the style and language of your report in keeping with the time the story was written.

2 Using an approach similar to *The Signalman*, write your own mystery story. Remember that effective description should be used, rather than gruesome details. It could be set somewhere such as a canal basin, an aerodrome or a disused mill.

   a) Use two characters – a narrator who visits the setting and a worker who has experienced fatal incidents and fears a third. Imagine you are the narrator.

b) Describe the location carefully, and the person who works there.

c) Let the worker relate the unusual incidents which have already occurred.

d) Include a third incident in which the worker's fears become a reality.

Explorations: comparing stories

1 From all the stories, choose the character whom you most admire and prepare a brief presentation explaining your choice. To make your selection you will need to consider such factors as the character's:

- situation
- actions
- personality
- relationship with others.

Be prepared to answer questions from the class about your choice.

2 Mathilde in *The Necklace* and Della and Jim in *The Gift of the Magi* have very different ways of looking at possessions and wealth. What do you think are the strengths and weaknesses of both points of view? Della and Jim delighted in giving each other their presents, proving the saying that it is often as pleasurable to give as to receive. Imagine you could give any present to someone close to you. Who would you choose? What would the gift be, and why would you choose it?

3 Look again at *An Alpine Divorce* and read carefully the description of the area in Switzerland which the Bodmans visited (pages 57–58). Design a postcard with a picture of the area and write the message as if you were one of the Bodmans' fellow guests. It could be written either before or after Mrs Bodman's death. Now look again at *The Parvenue* and write a postcard as if you were a fellow guest of

the narrator and her husband when they were abroad for two years (page 46). What similarities and differences might the guests observe in the characters and actions of the two women?

4 Think about:

- Mathilde in *The Necklace*
- the Sexton in *The Sexton's Hero*
- Jim in *The Gift of the Magi*
- the narrator in *The Parvenue*.

Imagine each of these characters could give one piece of advice to others after their experiences. What do you think it would be? The advice should be simple and reflect what they have learnt.

5 *An Alpine Divorce, The Thieves who Couldn't Help Sneezing* and *The Blue Carbuncle* are concerned with 'justice'. In groups, design a spider chart with 'justice' in the middle. Place around it all the associated words and phrases you can find, such as 'blind justice', 'justice of the peace', and so on. Record the meanings of the words and present your findings to the class.

6 In all the stories concerning 'justice', someone acted wrongly. Imagine you were the judge who had to hear the cases of Mr Bodman, the thieves who couldn't help sneezing and James Ryder. Prepare a short speech or written report explaining:

- what each person did wrong
- who, in your opinion, was guilty of the worst crime and why
- what 'just' punishment you think they deserve.

7 In *The Monkey's Paw*, the paw proves to be a token of bad luck or misfortune for the Whites. The appearance of the ghost in *The Signalman* fills the signalman with foreboding and fear. Using a table like the one below, find out about other tokens or actions which superstition says bring bad or good luck.

Bad luck	Good luck
Walking under a ladder	Black cat crossing your path

8 In *The Monkey's Paw*, *Napoleon and the Spectre* and *The Signalman* the authors build up suspense by using descriptive words and phrases which indicate that all is not well. Using a table like the one below, look at the opening of each story and note down words and phrases about:

- the surroundings in which the stories are set
- descriptions of the characters' actions and speech which show unease and foreboding.

Story	Setting	Character's action/speech
The Monkey's Paw	cold, wet night windy blinds drawn	grimly surveying (son) spoke with sudden, unlooked-for violence (Mr White)

Now write the opening of your own mystery story. Use descriptions of the setting and introduce the characters in a way that builds up suspense.

Coursework

1 Choose the story which you most enjoyed in this book. Write a review, explaining the reasons for your choice. You might like to consider the:

- opening
- setting
- main characters
- plot
- language
- ending.

Give examples from the text to support your comments where appropriate.

2 Look again at *The Necklace*, *The Sexton's Hero*, *The Gift of the Magi* and *The Parvenue*. Take each main character in turn and explain:

- what they thought most valuable in life
- your opinion of their values.

End with a comparison of what you consider to be most valuable or important in life.

3 *The Necklace* and *An Alpine Divorce* both feature women in difficult situations. Explain:

- Mathilde and Mrs Bodman's situations
- how each resolved their difficulties.

In what ways are the women's characteristics similar or different?

4 For some of the characters in the story you may feel sympathy, for others you may feel dislike – antipathy. Using a table like the one below, give your reaction to each character and a concise reason to support your choice. In pairs, compare your tables and discuss your differences.

	Sympathy	Antipathy	Reason
Mathilde			
Mrs White			
The Parvenue			
The Sexton			
Della			
Mr Bodman			
Bonaparte			

5 When their stories began, Mathilde, Mr Bodman and the Whites were all dissatisfied with their lives. Explain why each was dissatisfied and how they tried to improve their situation.

6 Imagine Mathilde, Mr Bodman and the Whites were to meet after their experiences. Write down what each might tell the others about:

- their regrets
- what they have learned
- how they have changed.

7 Look at the female characters in the stories: Mathilde, Della, the Parvenue, Mrs Bodman and Mrs White. Who do you think was the strongest and the weakest character?

a) Consider their:

- situations
- personal qualities
- decisions.

Can you see any strengths in the people you consider to be weak?

b) Look at the descriptive words and phrases used about the female characters you believe to be strongest and weakest. Has the author chosen words or phrases which support or influence your decision? Draw up a table like the one below to record your findings.

	Words used	**Resulting impression**
Strongest character e.g. Mrs Bodman	'usual hardness' (p.61) 'mad woman' (p.62) 'precipitated herself' (p.62)	tough, resilient dangerous brave
Weakest character e.g. Mathilde	'fretted constantly' (p.2) 'hopeless longing' (p.2)	dissatisfied unhappy

You may wish to compile a similar table for the strongest and weakest male characters.

8 Which 'mystery' story did you find most effective?
Consider their:

- themes
- settings
- characters
- language.

Support your comments with evidence from the
text.

Extension

1 Compare Gilbert Dawson in *The Sexton's Hero* with either Papa or Cassie Logan in *Roll of Thunder, Hear my Cry* or Atticus Finch in *To Kill a Mockingbird*. Consider their heroic qualities as seen in their:

- actions
- beliefs
- treatment of others.

2 In *The Gift of the Magi* Della and Jim clearly love each other dearly.

a) Describe how the story reveals their love.

b) Now read the poems *The Lowest Trees Have Tops* by Sir Edward Dyer and *Stop all the Clocks* by W H Auden.

Explain how love is portrayed in these poems by looking at the content and language.

c) Which of the three texts do you think is the best example of true love? Why? Explain your answer clearly.

3 In *The Parvenue* the narrator's mother was clearly a great influence on her daughter. Seamus Heaney wrote about his father in his poem *Follower*. Consider the two relationships and explain:

- the character and skills of both parents

- their children's attitudes toward them
- how the parents influenced their children.

Support your comments with examples from the text.

4 After reading *The Parvenue* and considering the character and situation of the narrator, read the play *Hobson's Choice* by Harold Brighouse which concerns another female as the main character.

- In what ways are the two women in similar situations?
- How does each react?
- What factors influence their decisions?
- What is your opinion of each woman?

5 *The Parvenue* and *An Alpine Divorce* show two women coping with difficult situations.

  a) Look at Maya Angelou's poem *Life Doesn't Frighten Me*.

  - What difficulties does the person in the poem face?
  - How does she cope with them?
  - What is your reaction to the way she copes?

  b) How does the person in the poem compare with the narrator of *The Parvenue* and Mrs Bodman?

6 After reading *An Alpine Divorce*, look at the short story *Turned* by Charlotte Perkins Gilman. Consider how the female characters both outwit their husbands after unhappy developments. You might like to consider:

- their dissatisfactions
- their characters
- their actions to retrieve the situation
- your opinions of the two women.

7 Read another of Sir Arthur Conan Doyle's 'Sherlock Holmes' stories, such as *The Speckled Band* or *The Hound of the Baskervilles*. Then watch a television or film version of any one of his exploits.

a) How do you react to the media's portrayal of Sherlock Holmes? You might like to think about his:

- physical appearance
- character and mannerisms
- method of detection.

b) Do you find the original stories or the media versions most convincing and interesting? Give reasons for your answers, using details from the text and film version to support your views.

Note: The Hound of the Baskervilles *and* Sherlock Holmes Faces Death *are available from Fox Video,* Sherlock Holmes and the Leading Lady *is available from Polygram, and* Sherlock Holmes *is available from Paradox films.*

8 After reading *Napoleon and the Spectre*, read *A Christmas Carol* by Charles Dickens.

- Select the words used by Charlotte Brontë to describe the spectre 'Piche', and explain what you think he wanted to show about Napoleon.
- Select words or phrases used by Charles Dickens to describe each of his spectres and explain what they wanted to show Scrooge.

Were the intentions of Napoleon's and Scrooge's spectres similar in any way?

Explain which spectre you found most threatening and why.

ALSO IN

HEINEMANN
NEW WINDMILLS

Founding Editors: Anne and Ian Serraillier

Chinua Achebe Things Fall Apart
Vivien Alcock The Cuckoo Sister; The Monster Garden;
The Trial of Anna Cotman; A Kind of Thief; Ghostly Companions
Margaret Atwood The Handmaid's Tale
Jane Austen Pride and Prejudice
J G Ballard Empire of the Sun
Nina Bawden The Witch's Daughter; A Handful of Thieves; Carrie's
War; The Robbers; Devil by the Sea; Kept in the Dark; The Finding;
Keeping Henry; Humbug; The Outside Child
Valerie Bierman No More School
Melvin Burgess An Angel for May
Ray Bradbury The Golden Apples of the Sun; The Illustrated Man
Betsy Byars The Midnight Fox; Goodbye, Chicken Little; The
Pinballs; The Not-Just-Anybody Family; The Eighteenth Emergency
Victor Canning The Runaways; Flight of the Grey Goose
Ann Coburn Welcome to the Real World
Hannah Cole Bring in the Spring
Jane Leslie Conly Racso and the Rats of NIMH
Robert Cormier We All Fall Down; Tunes for Bears to Dance to
Roald Dahl Danny, The Champion of the World; The Wonderful
Story of Henry Sugar; George's Marvellous Medicine; The BFG;
The Witches; Boy; Going Solo; Matilda
Anita Desai The Village by the Sea
Charles Dickens A Christmas Carol; Great Expectations;
Hard Times; Oliver Twist; A Charles Dickens Selection
Peter Dickinson Merlin Dreams
Berlie Doherty Granny was a Buffer Girl; Street Child
Roddy Doyle Paddy Clarke Ha Ha Ha
Gerald Durrell My Family and Other Animals
Anne Fine The Granny Project
Anne Frank The Diary of Anne Frank
Leon Garfield Six Apprentices; Six Shakespeare Stories;
Six More Shakespeare Stories
Jamila Gavin The Wheel of Surya
Adele Geras Snapshots of Paradise

Alan Gibbons Chicken
Graham Greene The Third Man and The Fallen Idol; Brighton Rock
Thomas Hardy The Withered Arm and Other Wessex Tales
L P Hartley The Go-Between
Ernest Hemmingway The Old Man and the Sea; A Farewell to Arms
Nigel Hinton Getting Free; Buddy; Buddy's Song
Anne Holm I Am David
Janni Howker Badger on the Barge; Isaac Campion; Martin Farrell
Jennifer Johnston Shadows on Our Skin
Toeckey Jones Go Well, Stay Well
Geraldine Kaye Comfort Herself; A Breath of Fresh Air
Clive King Me and My Million
Dick King-Smith The Sheep-Pig
Daniel Keyes Flowers for Algernon
Elizabeth Laird Red Sky in the Morning; Kiss the Dust
D H Lawrence The Fox and The Virgin and the Gypsy;
Selected Tales
Harper Lee To Kill a Mockingbird
Ursula Le Guin A Wizard of Earthsea
Julius Lester Basketball Game
C Day Lewis The Otterbury Incident
David Line Run for Your Life
Joan Lingard Across the Barricades; Into Exile; The Clearance;
The File on Fraulein Berg
Robin Lister The Odyssey
Penelope Lively The Ghost of Thomas Kempe
Jack London The Call of the Wild; White Fang
Bernard Mac Laverty Cal; The Best of Bernard Mac Laverty
Margaret Mahy The Haunting
Jan Mark Do You Read Me? (Eight Short Stories)
James Vance Marshall Walkabout
W Somerset Maughan The Kite and Other Stories
Ian McEwan The Daydreamer; A Child in Time
Pat Moon The Spying Game
Michael Morpurgo Waiting for Anya; My Friend Walter;
The War of Jenkins' Ear
Bill Naughton The Goalkeeper's Revenge
New Windmill A Charles Dickens Selection
New Windmill Book of Classic Short Stories
New Windmill Book of Nineteenth Century Short Stories

How many have you read?